The Trance Girl

The One Who Became an Addiction

ARJUN PRASANNAN

Chennai • Bangalore

CLEVER FOX PUBLISHING
Chennai, India

Published by CLEVER FOX PUBLISHING 2024
Copyright © Arjun Prasannan 2024

All Rights Reserved.
ISBN: 978-93-56485-35-8

This book has been published with all reasonable efforts taken to make the material error-free after the consent of the author. No part of this book shall be used, reproduced in any manner whatsoever without written permission from the author, except in the case of brief quotations embodied in critical articles and reviews.

The Author of this book is solely responsible and liable for its content including but not limited to the views, representations, descriptions, statements, information, opinions and references ["Content"]. The Content of this book shall not constitute or be construed or deemed to reflect the opinion or expression of the Publisher or Editor. Neither the Publisher nor Editor endorse or approve the Content of this book or guarantee the reliability, accuracy or completeness of the Content published herein and do not make any representations or warranties of any kind, express or implied, including but not limited to the implied warranties of merchantability, fitness for a particular purpose. The Publisher and Editor shall not be liable whatsoever for any errors, omissions, whether such errors or omissions result from negligence, accident, or any other cause or claims for loss or damages of any kind, including without limitation, indirect or consequential loss or damage arising out of use, inability to use, or about the reliability, accuracy or sufficiency of the information contained in this book.

This is for you, Dad!

Thank you for always being there through thick and thin.

Dedicated to her

The one who sells dreams is a writer.
When you are selling dreams, why not sell the most
"beautiful dream"?

CONTENTS

Preface ix
Acknowledgement x

1. Genesis Of Spring 1
2. Evocative Memories 4
3. The Woman In White 11
4. Magic Begins 15
5. Tale Of A Pasta 22
6. A Peck On The Cheek 35
7. Within The Hand's Reach 42
8. Before Sunrise 47
9. Embrace Your Desire 53
10. Celebration Of Life 60
11. Cheers To Montreal 71
12. Lucky Break 76
13. A Tale Of Two Cities 87
14. Ethereal Florence 94
15. Pleasant Surprise 108

Contents

16. The Art And The Artist 111
17. Red Rose Gardens 118
18. A Beacon Of Light 128
19. Last Painting 133
20. The Greatest Prayer 140

PREFACE

*I*n one of the campus chilling sessions at the Indian Institute of Management, Bangalore, one of my close friends shared a romantic encounter he had with a magical girl he met while on a student exchange program in Montreal at the age of 19. Intrigued, I asked what made her so special. "She had the most beautiful smile I had seen in the world", he replied. This piqued my curiosity even further.

He recounted how, during one of their late-night walks in Montreal, this enchanting young woman who had the most beautiful smile shared a deeply emotional experience with him. It was in that moment that he realized she possessed not only the most beautiful smile but also the most beautiful tears he had ever encountered. "The Trance Girl" was born then and there!

ACKNOWLEDGEMENT

$\mathcal{D}$rawing inspiration from real-life incidents, "The Trance Girl" was conceived and written in a myriad of unconventional settings over months and years. These included moving lifts, cars, fast-paced European trains, mundane meeting halls, rustic shacks on tranquil Goan beaches, and the majestic peaks of the Western Ghats. But in most cases, I found solace in writing in closed private rooms. The writing process was equally varied, spanning from digital platforms like Google Keep to the backside of bills and tissue papers, as well as the traditional pen and paper, and the all-time trusty and comfortable MacBook Air.

CHAPTER ONE

GENESIS OF SPRING

*M*arch 21st marked the beginning of the spring season of this year, 2019, in the ethereal city of Florence, a city of dreams and love. The sky appeared a shade bluer, untouched by the blossoms from the cherry trees that had not yet fallen onto the grey pavement. Spring's gentle touch is melting the last remnants of winter's chill, awakening the world from its slumber.

Florence is situated in central Italy and is decorated as the birthplace of the Renaissance. This "Athens of the Middle Ages" marked the rebirth of Western Civilisation. Located in the picturesque region of Tuscany, art, philosophy, literature, architecture, politics, and whatnot, every field was reborn and reinvented here. One of the most iconic landmarks in Florence is the Cathedral of Santa Maria del Fiore, known for its magnificent dome designed by Filippo Brunelleschi. The city is also home to the Uffizi Gallery, which houses a vast collection of Renaissance art, including works by Leonardo da Vinci, Michelangelo, and Botticelli. Florence's charm extends beyond its artistic treasures. The city's winding streets are lined with quaint cafes, boutiques, and gelaterias, creating a romantic atmosphere perfect for leisurely strolls. The Ponte Vecchio, a medieval stone bridge spanning the Arno River, is a popular spot for couples to enjoy panoramic views of the city and watch the sunset.

Life was indeed a celebration in this city for years, precisely visible in every nook and corner. The Florence city centre is flooded with moving people, sipping red wine, enjoying the music and dance street performances, and admiring the beauty of the paramount Roman architecture in the form of arches and domes. This city served as a fantasy for the couples, who were essentially living a dream. No wonder why Italy summoned the largest inflow of tourists in the world.

In a bustling Florence café, Akshay, a sturdy young man in his late twenties, sat waiting for his pre-ordered pasta, his expression clouded with longing and loss. Despite his successful career as a management consultant in Europe, a loving family in Chennai, and a close-knit group of friends, Akshay found himself grappling with the absence of something precious—a captivating smile, now lost to him.

Every day, Akshay sought solace in the familiar ritual of ordering Pappardelle in wild boar Ragu, a Tuscan delicacy. With its rustic texture, this long, wide pasta had become a comfort, offering a taste of familiarity in a world that felt increasingly foreign. Born and raised on the flavours of sambar rice and curd rice in South India, Akshay had embarked on a remarkable journey—one that had not only broadened his culinary horizons but also deepened his sense of longing for the smile that once lit up his world.

This particular Italian pasta served as a poignant reminder for Akshay, evoking memories of a vibrant and transformative period in his life—the sixty days he spent in Montreal, Canada, as part of his undergraduate research internship program. As he savoured each bite of the Pappardelle, Akshay found himself transported back to a time of exploration and discovery, captured in the photos he had taken during the closing days of his teenage years in Canada.

As his European project approached its conclusion, Akshay found himself in Florence for the last few weeks before heading back to Kochi city in India for his cousin's wedding. Despite the imminent arrival of his pasta, Akshay abruptly stood from his chair, made his way to the exit, discarded the flower bouquet to his right, and proceeded to the nearest metro stop. Although his consulting firm would cover his food expenses, leaving his meal unfinished seemed out of character. Could this impulsive departure be a sign of someone deeply preoccupied with a search, perhaps for someone special?

As Akshay exited the café, a woman and an eight-year-old girl took his place. They ordered two plates of Pappardelle in wild boar Ragu and settled in. The girl eagerly opened her neatly wrapped diary, which she always carried, and began sketching. She had a unique hobby of creating pencil sketches of memorable moments. After a few minutes, she turned the diary around to show her companion a portrait she had just completed. It was a beautiful, graceful smile—the very same kind of smile that Akshay had been searching for. As the woman looked at the sketch, her face lit up with a radiant smile reminiscent of what Akshay longed to find.

CHAPTER TWO

EVOCATIVE MEMORIES

Akshay's consulting project in Florence was towards its closure. He was staffed on an assignment whose main objective was to improve the tourism revenue of the Tuscany region. Apart from delving into his professional project, this stunning city, with its fascinating culture of art and history, has transported Akshay to a whole new space. The riverside of the Arno River, the busy shopping streets of the iconic medieval stone arch bridge, *Ponte Vecchio*, and the city landscape at Piazzale Michelangelo take away your breath throughout the day. However, the city faced a significant decline in tourism revenue for three to four years, forcing the authorities to hire a consulting firm and suggest feasible solutions. Akshay and his team of eight people have been working on this project for the past four months. They have devised numerous strategies on paper, such as bundling entry fees for different tourist attractions as combined packages, reallocating street shops with lesser competition, and targeting promotions and advertising during the peak seasons and holidays.

The implementation phase would be constituted by a separate team, which should be started after the ideation plan is approved.

Today, Akshay and his team have the third review meeting with his client, consisting of Florence government officials and administrators. He entered the Florence administration building in his routine costume of a white-coloured shirt, waistcoat, red-coloured tie, and well-waxed and polished dark-coloured leather shoes. He meets his colleague Madhu and discusses the final presentation and recent updates from the late-night discussions with their senior team. Contrary to the characteristics of the guy who waited indefinitely inside the café a few days back, a career-oriented, confident, and focused Akshay is now seen. The presentation went decently with many more changes and suggestions, which means his Florence days will be a week longer.

The day is about to be over. Florentine sunsets are breathtaking, tinted with a magical perspire of the land. These remarkable sunsets can be ideally viewed from three different locations. The first would be gazing at the sunset after climbing the four hundred steps to the top of the Duomo. This magnificent cathedral offers an adventurous view of the sunset, and the last of the warm rays bounce off an endless sea of red on Tuscan rooftops, which is absorbingly calming. The second option would be near the Arno River, which becomes a mass of fiery red and orange houses as the Sun descents. The traditional boat named a *barchetto* will blissfully guide you across the river, and arranging a bottle of wine can be the extra topping for an unforgettable romantic experience. The third and the last option is the most unmissable and, not surprisingly, the most popular Piazzale Michelangelo. This charismatic square that offers a panoramic view of the city and embraces the sunset in its full glory is reserved for the climax portion of the tale of Akshay.

Akshay's team decided to leave the office early today as they were exhausted from the consecutive working days. Meanwhile, Madhu messaged Akshay from one corner of the room to the other. "When will you be free today? Let's catch up in the evening"?

"Sounds difficult. I will be late". Akshay texted back.

Hours passed on. Akshay felt exhausted from the hectic day and reconsidered Madhu's evening plan at Café Rossano at 10:30 pm. Café Rossano is a gem of a Café. The delicious pistachio croissants served by the friendly and warm staff, along with the world's best coffee in the form of soy in cappuccino, is an offer that none can refuse.

"Sure. I hope we get a table". Madhu agreed to the plan.

"That's sorted. I know a bartender working in Rossano. He will reserve a table for us".

Jai Kishan was Akshay's childhood buddy who dropped out of 12th standard and migrated to Europe with his uncle, the chief chef in Amsterdam's five-star hotels. After leaving India, he transformed himself from the Desi "Jai Kishan" version to the stylish "Jackie".

"Hey, Jackie! Reserve two seats for me tonight". Akshay calls his friend Jai Kishan, aka Jackie, the bartender.

Jackie: "Woah! Who is getting lucky tonight"?

"Idiot"! Akshay smiles and replies. "Tell me, dude". Jackie got curious.

"We will be there by 10:30 pm. Reserve a seat near a corner. I would prefer a private conversation".

"Sure, boss", Jackie replied back.

Around 9:30 pm, Akshay picks up Madhu from her hotel in a shared cab. She looks gorgeous in a violet gown and a pearl embroidered silver chain. "Why are you dressed up"? Akshay was surprised.

"Aren't we visiting a café in Florence, Europe? So, I think it is justifiable". Akshay was not convinced and continued his focus on the journey.

Moreover, my grandma always used to say, "Even a corpse should be well dressed. Maybe I inherited that trait, and now it's a habit…" Madhu continued her preaching, and Akshay replied with a smile before he spoke.

Akshay: "It's been a month since we have met, right"?

Madhu: "Yes. Close to a month".

Akshay: "Seems like we knew each other forever".

Madhu: "Hmm, yeah".

Akshay: "I can feel a connection drawing us in".

Madhu doesn't reply.

Akshay: "Do you not"?

Madhu: "In this fast-moving world, one month is more than enough for two people to connect. Or instead, I feel it's too long".

Akshay tilted his head towards Madhu, smiled, and asked, "Seriously"? Madhu also tilts her head towards Akshay, smiles, and confirms, "Yes". Both laugh and the driver replies that they have reached their destination.

"Come, let's move in", Madhu says, and Akshay follows her. They see a crowded café with just a seat in the centre unoccupied as they enter. "Is this his private seat"? Akshay murmured in anger and hunts for Jackie around. Jackie displays a thump from a distant corner while busily serving beer individually. "Idiot"!. Akshay curses him.

"What happened"? Madhu wondered.

"Ahh, nothing". They took their seat and ordered pizzas, fettunta (garlic bread), crostini Neri (chicken liver pate served on toast), and two bottles of red wine. They continued conversing about the hectic days, cribbing on the late-night assignments, and effectively using the European days left.

Madhu: "Hardly ten days left in Europe now. How about extending the stay here for another ten days and going to Europe backpacking"?

Akshay: "Where do you want to go? I have my cousin's marriage scheduled in a few weeks".

Madhu: "That's fine. It would be at most ten days when we can visit London, Paris and maybe Budapest. I have heard Budapest is lovely and cheap. Backpacking in Europe has been on my bucket list for a long time. One of my close friends works with Amazon in London; we can crash at her place, and she will take us around. It can cut a lot of travel expenses".

Akshay was lost somewhere. Madhu noticed his disinterest in her exciting adventure plans.

"Do you want to have a beer"? Akshay spoke after a while.

"No. I am good. What's bothering you, Akshay? Is it the work pressure"? Akshay didn't reply to Madhu but ordered a beer. Madhu gets agitated and starts checking her phone. Akshay chugs one more beer.

"What happened to you, man? Come on! I won't be judgmental". Madhu enquired.

"Madhu, I am in deep distress. I am unsure if you would understand the depth of what I am saying; I wanted to share a pain with you, a pain I have been carrying around for years. I thought I could get relieved of it in this Florence journey, but it looks difficult. I need help. Can you help me escape from this"? Akshay took a pause and then continued.

"The pain of happiness, the pain of hope, and the pain of love".

"Sure, Akshay. I assure you my help". Madhu got excited and assumed to hear another heartbreak story from Akshay.

"Madhu, I had a hidden agenda in joining this project in Florence. If you remember, I had to convince the engagement manager multiple times to shift me from the Mumbai offshore project. It was an arduous task. I went through all that in the hope of meeting her here. It's been seven years and ten months that I have seen her. This was my last hope of meeting her again. Every day, I searched for her through various means. I enquired about all the flower business groups in Florence, as well as different retail shops and Indian communities. Unfortunately, nothing has worked so far, and now I can't imagine leaving this city without meeting her"! Madhu was confused. She hardly understood what he said, apart from the fact that he was passionately searching for someone.

"Akshay, I empathize with your feelings, but can you explain the context a bit more so we can work together to find your girl"? Madhu sounded formal and objective to seek clarity in Akshay's communication.

Madhu picks up a pack of the legendary Tuscan Cigar she procured and shares one with Akshay. Akshay lights the roll, which is made of high-quality fermented Kentucky Tobacco. The smokes fill the air and dissipate into thin air, only to take the time backward.

Year rewinds to 2011, the month to May, the day to 6[th,] and the location shifts to Chennai, India, and precisely the rooftop of Jamuna Hostel, Indian Institute of Technology, Madras.

CHAPTER THREE

THE WOMAN IN WHITE

Chennai, located in Southern India, is known for its rich cultural heritage, white sand beaches, and an umpteen variety of seafood. The bustling streets of Chennai, filled with the aroma of local delicacies like dosas and filter coffee, offer a sensory experience that immerses the characters and readers alike in the city's unique ambience. One of the oldest cities in the country, it boasts many unique distinctions like the capital city of the birthplace of the oldest language in the world (*Tamil*), the second-longest coastline (*Marina Beach*), the birthplace of the classic spicy deep-fried chicken dish, Chicken 65 and houses the oldest Engineering college in Asia (*College of Engineering, Guindy*).

Opposite this oldest engineering college lies the main gate of Akshay's campus. The college hostels are named after the perennially rich rivers of India, and he occupied the Jamuna hostel, named after the Jamuna River. IITs are popularly known for the difficulty of their entrance examination and the elite social status enjoyed by the students, teachers, and alums. However, the campus' turbulent hostel terraces call for a festival if there is a reason to celebrate among the inmates. Glittering illuminations, decorative items, a drinking counter, a smoking arena, umpteen sheets of rolling paper, two-three bongs, and a seductive dope, this list constituted a regular terrace party. The incumbent reason was Akshay, a Chemical Engineering sophomore at IIT Madras, departure to Canada for two months as a part of the research internship program. Akshay was one of the three selected from the campus for the prestigious MITACS research scholarship to various Canadian universities. He was the only one chosen to the University of Montreal, and his wingmates had organised a farewell party for him that night. At the hostel terrace, we could spot his friends engaged in different affairs; Aravind rolling a joint with utmost proficiency, Madhav playing "*Hotel California*" on his acoustic guitar, and Thomas was busy refining the hostel décor. When Aravind was about to light the joint, Thomas intervened and asked Akshay to light it and begin the celebration. Akshay lights the joint and coughs badly. Akshay, an introvert, was premature at parties and was tensed about traveling to a foreign country alone. It was his first foreign trip, and he had to travel alone. His friends were also concerned about how a naïve teenager like Akshay would survive within the Western lifestyle. Some of the self-proclaimed swaggers wished they had received Akshay's opportunity.

The night went longer with more lights, lighting, ashes, smoke, and drinks. Akshay gradually got intoxicated, and the irregular mixing of intoxications had its unique and strange intensity. Akshay relaxed his consciousness, proffered it complete independence, and lay down on the terrace. It was a full moon night, but the clouds were densely turbulent, concealing the moon on and off. Akshay pondered deep into the uninterrupted cat-and-mouse game of the clouds and moon. Slowly, he got engulfed in this bizarre game and was taken to a misty, dreamy world where he was lost alone in a hostel kitchen. He saw many students cooking themselves the food they chose; some cooked idli, others made Maggi noodles, some made shawarma, and others made Marconi.

"Wait, what a combo is that"? Akshay wondered!

He continued hopping through the kitchen and observed the various food packets of basmati rice, mayonnaise, instant coffee powder, soya sauce, sausages, and bread packets. Akshay then moved out of the kitchen and explored the hostel amenities. The hostel had a playroom where students played indoor carroms, UNO card games, and handballs on the outer ground. He also noticed a pretty girl reading the 1859 classic mysterious novel "The Woman in White" by Wilkie Collins resting on the sofa. Akshay heard some strange noise in the outer ground and rushed outside in enthusiasm but in vain. "What sound was that"? Akshay wondered. He walked further. As Akshay took further steps, the misty clouds became more evident, and the sight was better. Akshay saw a girl in a white t-shirt and blue jeans in her late teenage years staring at the moon with better vision. Her face was not visible, but she appeared beautiful and stayed alone. With tremendous enthusiasm, Akshay went ahead, intending to strike up a conversation.

"Hey"! She turned back, and instantly, Akshay heard the sound of a breaking glass bottle.

"Damn! That's a full Bacardi bottle aimlessly lying on the floor"! Varun, Akshay's friend, exclaimed.

Reality reclaimed its hold, but Akshay remained adrift in dreams. Who was that girl standing outside the hostel room? Shaking off the reverie, he returned to his room to complete the final packing before his flight in a few short hours. Three suitcases filled, he thanked his friends for the heartfelt farewell party, bid goodbye, and headed to Chennai International Airport in a cab.

Each taxi ride from the hostel triggered memories. The first was a joyous journey to IIT Madras from the Chennai railway station at the start of his first semester. However, the thought of the final cab ride he would take upon graduation two years hence filled him with unease. These past two years, he had been the highlight of his life. Could life possibly get any better? Akshay often pondered. Little did he know the next two months in Montreal would hold surprises that would forever change his life.

CHAPTER FOUR

MAGIC BEGINS

*A*fter more than twenty hours of strenuous journey, Akshay landed at the Montreal International Airport. Montreal, located in the Quebec province of Canada, is the second-most populous city in the country. Originally titled the "City of Mary", it was later renamed after Mont-Royal, the triple-peaked hill located in the city's heart.

Montreal-Pierre Elliott Trudeau International Airport, commonly known as Montreal Airport, stood as a miracle to Akshay, who believed the Chennai International Airport was one of the best globally. The airport's setting provided a rich backdrop for a story, offering a mix of modernity and cultural charm. As travellers approached the airport, they were greeted by sleek, contemporary architecture that reflected Montreal's status as a cosmopolitan city. The airport's design featured large windows that allowed natural light to flood the terminals, creating a sense of openness and space. Art installations and exhibits showcasing local artists and culture were scattered throughout the terminals, giving travellers a taste of Montreal's vibrant arts scene. Restaurants and cafes offered a variety of regional and international cuisine, allowing travellers to indulge in Montreal's culinary delights before or after their journey. The sound of different languages filled the air, adding to the airport's lively and cosmopolitan atmosphere.

He also noticed a sharp decrease in temperature by around 20 degrees Celsius between the two cities. Amongst these diverse thoughts, he almost got lost in figuring out a way to pick up his check-in luggage before he received a call from behind.

"Hey, Bro!"! Akshay turned back. He spotted another teenager happily rushing towards him.

"What's up? Which college are you heading to"? The teenager in a black overcoat raised a query.

"Hi, I am heading to the University of Montreal", Akshay replied to the enthusiastic chap.

"Great, I am also heading there. My name is Abhinav". He extended his hands for a warm and confident shake.

"Hey, nice to meet you, Abhinav. I am Akshay, from IIT Madras, and you are from which college"?

"I am from NIT Trichy". Abhinav's college, National Institute of Technology, Trichy, was another premier engineering college located roughly 340 km South of IIT Madras.

"Nice. Which city are you flying from"? Akshay wondered why he hadn't noticed Abhinav before his flight.

"I flew from Mumbai now, but my parents stay in Hyderabad. And what about you"? Abhinav clarified Akshay's query.

"I am originally from Kochi, Kerala, but boarded the flight from Chennai directly from campus".

Abhinav: "Nice; I love Kerala and the food. Especially the seafood and the mouthwatering beef".

Akshay: "Yeah, that's the most common compliment I get. Meanwhile, do you know where to collect the luggage from"?

Abhinav: "Yes, it is counter 11; come, I will take you".

Akshay felt relieved to meet Abhinav; he hoped Abhinav would help collect his luggage and be potentially good company for the next two months. From counter 11, they collected the bag, prebooked a taxi, and moved out of the airport. Montreal was magnificent to Akshay. The city bestowed only good vibes to Akshay with a well-organised parking space, luxurious taxi cabs, wide roads, no long waiting at traffic signals, and well-defined signboards. They travelled nearly twenty kilometres in less than fifteen minutes and reached the university entrance. Akshay noticed the university buildings, which were huge and more well-built than his home college. Nestled on the slopes of Mount Royal, the University's campus boasted a picturesque setting, with historic buildings and modern facilities blending seamlessly into the lush greenery of the mountain. As Akshay navigated the campus, he encountered a vibrant tapestry of cultures and ideas reflective of Montreal's diverse population. Still, he badly missed the greenery of IIT Madras, the campus carved out of Guindy National Park, where human beings, monkeys, blackbucks, and a large variety of wildlife co-existed peacefully.

As soon as they reached the campus, they had an orientation session in the evening. Established in 1878, this French-language public research university currently constituted thirty-four thousand undergraduate and eleven thousand post-graduate students across sixty departments, almost three times the size of IIT Madras. After the orientation, they had a couple of informal interactive sessions with faculty and students to learn more about the campus. The first week constituted various ice-breaking sessions, fun activities, sports sessions, and cultural performances, which were enlisted in a tabular format. Abhinav met a Spanish girl named Debora during the orientation week and spent the following days with her, which led to more loneliness for Akshay. Akshay enjoyed the orientation activities and made a few connections, but he couldn't relate to anyone meaningfully. Rather than faking himself, he focused on academic research and leisure activities. The Montreal world appeared so vast to him that he believed no one cared for him there, nor did he care for anyone. A week passed at full tilt for Abhinav and steadily for Akshay.

The following Sunday, both were together in the hostel room and decided to head for dinner to the hostel mess. On the way, they noticed the campus premises preparing for a thespian performance. Abhinav became interested in the stage decorations, which consisted of the performers dressed in black clothes, maple leaves, hockey sticks, and brown vintage jackets as props. The combo looked strange to him. Abhinav wanted to explore the drama more, but Akshay convinced him to look at the performance after having dinner. However, when they returned twenty minutes after the meal, the place was crowded with hundreds of students.

"Come, Akshay. This looks promising". Abhinav ran towards the performance in excitement. At the same time, Akshay walked further slowly with a plugged-in earphone. As he moved closer, he realised he lost Abhinav in the crowd and dropped his earphones to listen to the drama.

"Grele compatriots", the crowd shouted in French.

Owing to the language barrier, Akshay chose the music playlist on his phone over the street play while keeping his eyes alert on the performance. Six performers moved around the centre of the play arena, surrounded by a large crowd, cheering and listening to their performance. Akshay spotted a beautiful smile from the opposite side through that thickly populated crowd while listening to a piece of good music on his earphones. He could hardly see her as her face got lost between the moving group. Upon seeing her smile, Akshay removed his earphones and walked hastily in search of that smile. The street play was nearing its end, and he realised that the climax orchestra music played was entrancing to the ears. But the girl was lost in the crowd; the music ended abruptly, and people dispersed quickly. The gathering took her away. Nevertheless, there was something magical about her smile, and Akshay felt motivated to hunt for the owner in the subsequent days. Akshay returned to the hostel room with swerving thoughts and forgot about Abhinav, who was also lost in the crowd.

Early in the morning, around 5:30 am, Akshay got a call on his phone while sleeping. The call got disconnected in two dials, and it was an unknown number. He then realised that he had lost Abhinav on the way and had not returned to their room yet. Akshay comfortably assumed Abhinav would have gone to meet Debora. Within a few minutes, he received the call from the unknown number again, and the Truecaller's notification indicated the name Debora. He dialled back to both the numbers but in vain. Finally, he decided to go to Debora's room in search of Abhinav.

Debora's block was a five minutes' walk from his room. He traversed through the peaceful walkways of the University and climbed the steps a level above room 132, Debora's room. He saw Abhinav lying on her bed, dead drunk.

"Hey, Akshay! Abhinav overshoots his drinks today. I am sorry, I need to leave home urgently now and can't take care of him. Can you please take him to his room"? Debora made a humble request to Akshay.

Akshay felt defenceless and useless in life at the same time. But he had no option; he assisted Abhinav on his shoulders and carried him towards their room. On the way, he noticed a girl locking the room, room number 135, and heading out. She wore a black t-shirt similar to the one worn by the girl he met in the street play that evening. He dropped Abhinav and followed her.

"Here I lie again", Abhinav wailed.

Akshay went closer to her and said, "Excuse me", to which she turned back with a tender smile. She was not the one. Akshay replied sorry and returned to Abhinav, who was comfortably lying on the verandah. Akshay picked him up again and slowly stepped to his place while the sun's rays of hope were bestowed on him.

CHAPTER FIVE

TALE OF A PASTA

"*A*kshay, wake up!"!Abhinav shouted. It was 9 in the morning, and Abhinav was getting ready for their morning class at 10 am.

"You are impossible. I just dropped you here a few hours back sloshed". Akshay was surprised at Abhinav, to which he just replied with a confident smirk.

After getting ready, they moved on to the mess for breakfast and to the auditorium for class. The days passed away usually. Since Debora was not in town, Abhinav spent his time with Akshay, and they roamed and went shopping in Montreal. They visited the botanical garden, the famous chapel Notre-Dame Basilica, the fine arts museum, and the Chinatown. Nestled on the island of Montreal along the St. Lawrence River, Akshay noticed the city to be a harmonious blend of old-world charm and modern sophistication.

Montreal's culinary scene is legendary, with a plethora of restaurants, cafes, and bistros offering a tantalizing array of cuisines. From classic French fare to innovative fusion dishes,

Montreal's food scene reflects its status as a culinary capital. In the shadow of Mount Royal, Montreal stands as a testament to the enduring spirit of its people. In this city, tradition and modernity coexist perfectly, creating a tapestry of experiences that captivate and inspire all who visit. The few days of travel were a fresh experience for Akshay before becoming occupied with his research work. There was a first draft deadline scheduled in a week, and Akshay focused on it. Another week passed, and altogether, it had been three weeks for Akshay and Abhinav in Montreal. It was time for another weekend party on campus. Abhinav was excited as usual, while Akshay was tired of the nightlife in three weeks.

"Dude, you should surely join today! It's going to be an exciting night"! Abhinav appeared more excited than his words.

"How is it, different man? You go there, drink like a fish, dance like a madman, and then return without consciousness. The worst part is you remember shit for the next day"! Akshay was crystal clear on his reasons for the denial.

"Tonight's more than what you told. Speed friending, fun games, and beer chugging competition. And you know, I met Debora at such a party! Who knows, you will also meet someone tonight"? But Abhinav's pitch was not attractive enough for Akshay, and he decided to stay back.

Akshay continued working on an assignment in his room. Boredom hit him hard. The master light in his room was not working. Moreover, he craved Indian food. So, he decided to inspect the hostel's common kitchen and see if he could afford to cook any simple dish like curd rice. Strangely, his hostel kitchen was locked from the outside. Akshay decided to check out the kitchens of adjacent hostels. The door of the next hostel kitchen he visited was wide open. Akshay moved in. It was empty except for a girl cooking something on the induction stove, and it smelled like pasta.

"Damn! How can someone cook pasta in a hostel kitchen when you get the same food in a hostel mess"? Akshay murmured.

Hearing Akshay's voice, she turned around and smiled at Akshay. This smile belonged to the girl he saw in the street play and whom he searched endlessly in the crowd. Akshay couldn't believe his eyes.

"Hey! Come in; I am almost done. Let me clear this space for you". The girl replied joyfully.

Akshay greeted her and moved closer to look at her dish. She kindly offered him the delicious hot pasta that she cooked. Akshay picked up a spoon and pushed it inside the plate to taste the pasta, but the girl interrupted and introduced herself, "Hi, I am Saesha". Her smile and reply almost fulfilled Akshay's food craving.

"Hello, Saesha, I am Akshay". Akshay dropped the spoon on the table to reply to her.

"Ohh, I am sorry; please go ahead with the pasta", Saesha replied.

Akshay, who was agnostic about the concepts of pasta and pizzas, felt that this pasta was different. It had a few unique flavours and was rightly cooked. "It's excellent"! Akshay complimented the dish and wanted to know what made it special.

"I know, right? You tasted Pappardelle, an authentic and classic Italian pasta". She was delighted to know that Akshay liked her dish.

"Have we met before"? Akshay wanted to converse more.

"Yes, I had noticed you during the street play a few days back. We had interlocked our eyes for a few seconds from opposite directions". She chuckled and continued. "I think I spotted you in some other places after that".

Akshay was surprised. She knows about him! Both continued munching the pasta while they conversed more. Saesha introduced her as an exchange student from the sociology department of Solvay Brussels School of Economics and Management, Belgium, selected as a part of the MITACS scholarship from her college.

"Are you an NRI (Non-Resident Indian), then"? Akshay doubted her nationality, though she had a name from the Indian subcontinent.

"I was born and brought up in Florence till my school education before shifting to Brussels for my undergraduate education. For decades, my family has run a floral wholesaling business in Europe, and we are settled in Florence".

"Damn! But why Florence? I think Paris would be a better place for the floral industry, right"? After replying, he wondered why he stressed the city aspect of her reply.

"You are right and wrong. Florence is in no way related to the flower industry. The business primarily lies within countries like the Netherlands and France. Have you heard of the small town of Aalsmeer in the Netherlands? The largest flower auction in the world is situated there, and that's where the actual money flows in". Saesha clarified his query.

"Then why are you settled in Florence"? Akshay became more baffled.

"What is the fun if I tell you everything about myself in one go"? She smiled. "Agreed". He agreed to disagree.

"Come on, how can you not introduce yourself"? Saesha tried changing the pursuing topic of discussion.

"I am nameless and shameless; my nick is". Akshay stopped his introduction in embarrassment.

"What! What was that"? Saesha felt strange. "I am sorry, that's the intro format used by seniors in IITM during the ragging session"? Akshay intervened for immediate clarity.

"What's IITM"? But Saesha was more curious.

"I am sorry, it is IIT Madras, Indian Institute of Technology, Madras, one of the top-ranked engineering colleges in India". Akshay wondered how she could be so ignorant in life but didn't express it. "I completed my second year and am here as a part of the MITACS scholarship as well", Akshay concluded with his explanation.

"That's nice. And I think you are a nerd then, excused this time". Saesha sarcastically consoled him. But Akshay expressed an upset face.

Saesha: "Hey! I was kidding, don't take it to heart, buddy"!

Akshay: "Yeah, I know. I am used to such tags now".

Saesha: "Come on, cheer up! Let's go for a walk".

Akshay: "Are you sure"?

Saesha: "Yes, why not"?

Akshay rolled up his brown jacket to withstand the night summers of Montreal. "Woah! You are looking smart, though it is not that cold outside". Saesha complimented Akshay, and he politely smiled.

Both exited the kitchen and walked through the well-paved, indefinite roads of the University. Akshay slowly started appreciating the beauty of this campus at the IIT Madras levels.

"Have you been to India"? Akshay interrupted the silence.

"Why do you think I am from India; do I look like an Indian"? Saesha raised her eyebrows and shifted her face towards Akshay. "Because you told me you are an NRI, a Non-Resident Indian". Akshay questioned her back firmly.

"I am sorry; I told you I was born and raised in Florence". She clarified herself again.

"But, I have a few relatives in India, and we visit them occasionally; now it's been pretty long".

"Where are you then originally from"? Akshay pushed back.

"Take a guess"! She paused in the walk and replied.

"My guess was India". Akshay also took a break from the walk.

"My parents are Sri Lankan natives who migrated to Europe during the civil war in the late 80s". Saesha continued walking and spoke. "That's quite impressive. Tell me more about it". Akshay followed her steps.

"So, you know, those were the days of civil war between the Tamils and the Sinhalese-speaking people of Sri Lanka supported by the Sri Lankan government. My father was a Tamilian, while my mother belonged to the Sinhalese community; they were college classmates. An unusual friendship that blossomed into love in the hardest of times. Being born in rival communities, they realised that the situation in Sri Lanka was highly unpleasant for them to unite. They jointly dreamt of a futuristic Sri Lanka without war, conflicts, and peace among all the communities. However, the situation only deteriorated in the later years. Finally, towards the end of graduation, they made plans to emigrate out of the country. Both were barely 20 then, almost our current age then.

"That's incredible"! Akshay exclaimed.

"My father had a friend working in Paris, and he secretly arranged a job visa for my parents. The lovely couple cutely absconded from their motherland. For the first few months, my parents worked hard under a flower wholesaler in Paris and decided to onboard enough savings before marriage. This beautiful continent made them dream big, first of marriage and later set up their own business. They choose the beautiful medieval city of Florence for their dream wedding. The wedding and the few post-wedding days spent in Florence inspired them to settle in that charming place in the future. With this determined mind, they worked day and night diligently and slowly ventured out their floral wholesaling in Amsterdam, which has grown to one of the largest in Europe now. And that's how we are settled in Florence while we manage businesses all over Europe".

"This story is nothing less of a fairytale. I hope you didn't mend a random story to bluff this middle-class Indian". Akshay startled.

"You don't trust me"? Saesha replied with a straight face.

"I am sorry, I didn't mean to".

Saesha browsed through her mobile phone gallery and shared a few photographs of their parent's wedding, floral farms, and the flower auction markets as proof. Akshay couldn't believe that he was conversing with a European billionaire!

Akshay: "Are you the only kid"?

Saesha: "Yes, I am".

Akshay: "Damn! I can't believe how lucky the person who would marry you is".

Saesha: "Why"?

Akshay: "Because you are filthy rich"!

Saesha: "That's my only worth"?

"I didn't mean it". He apologised again.

"Yeah, I know what you meant. I have also thought about it and have devised a plan to find my true love. I wouldn't express my personal life details to the guys I am interested in and continue dating them as a normal person. But, if we start developing feelings mutually, I will reveal my true nature; I want him to fall for me and not for my money".

"Interesting". Akshay thought for a while and then replied. "But you told me all the details about your personal life, so you are not at all interested in me, right"?

"How else could I have made it more precise"? Saesha replied in a serious tone to Akshay's innocent query.

"It makes sense; it is better to clarify things at the beginning itself", Akshay murmured again and walked hastily ahead. Saesha controlled her laughter and accompanied him.

"How do you find the city of Montreal? What all have you explored yet"? Saesha attempted to digress the conversation route again. "Just been to a few ordinary places like the museums, palaces, etc., along with a friend of mine, Abhinav".

"Why? Don't you have more friends here"?

"I met Abhinav on the first day in Montreal, and we quickly bonded. Then, I believed it would be easy to make friends here. But after that, I think you are the second person I have met whom I can probably count as a friend".

"Why only, probably"? She giggled. "We just met now". He delivered a serious look to which Saesha casually smiled.

Saesha: "Why don't you hang out with Abhinav, then"?

Akshay: "Yeah, we do at times. And that's how we visited all these places, but he spends more time with his Spanish girlfriend, Debora".

Saesha: "Woah. Did he start dating here"?

Akshay nodded yes.

"Why don't you try for a girlfriend here, or are you already taken"?

"No, I am single now. And I am telling you I am struggling to make friends here, and you are asking me to date someone? How cruel that is"?

Saesha laughed and continued, "Tell me your love story".

"Ahh, that's an old one. Maybe I will tell you the summary. We were in the same school; she joined my school on June 2nd, 2004. And it was the onset of the monsoon season in Kerala, my home state in India. The school reopens, and the beginning of the monsoon season coincide yearly; hence, we start every academic year on a rainy day. It rained, as usual, that day, and she came to our seventh standard classroom drenched in the rain with a blushed smile".

"That's a good build-up". Saesha got engrossed in Akshay's narration. "What was her name"?

"Her name was Mithila; she was smart, intelligent, and an all-rounder who excelled in academics, dance, music, and acting. She became the face of our school in all youth festivals, which motivated me to become the class leader. The class leader was responsible for bringing the team together for all competitions. Through these interactions, we became pretty close friends. Most evenings after the regular classes, she had practice sessions, and I used to wait until she finished. After her practice, we used to cycle back home together. This became a routine for a month. On one such evening, she was at her dance practice for the upcoming school cultural fest, and I secretly admired her from a distance. After the session, she rushed towards me to grab the water bottle and started sipping; then I told her".

"You proposed to her"? Saesha asked excitedly.

"I can't stop falling for you."

"I told her this, and she spat the water into my face", Akshay replied. Saesha laughed loudly.

"Yeah, now when I look back, it is funny. She didn't respond well, but I realised she enjoyed my company and started noticing my actions more often. We conversed through the landline for long hours; those were the days of the innocent and cute early teenage romance. We had telephonic code words like, 'science exam is postponed,' which meant parents are away from the phone, and 'science exam is tomorrow,' which meant parents are nearby". Akshay smiled nostalgically often while narrating his story.

"And where is she now"? Saesha stopped again out of curiosity. She also looked around to realise they had come a long way from the hostel.

"I joined the science stream in my eleventh standard, and she got shifted to another school. We were still in touch, but I had little time to invest in the relationship due to my hectic academic preparation for the engineering entrance examinations. Two years passed on. After finishing my entrance exams, I was entirely free for two solid months before joining IIT Madras. We started meeting again during the weekends, and the phone calls became more frequent except for the fact that we got upgraded from landlines to mobile phones. Slowly, I realised that we had changed; the last two years had changed our lifestyles, interests, and thoughts. She appeared like a whole new person to me, but I hid all those emotions from her, as I still wanted to have her in my life. But it worsened after I joined IIT Madras, and she joined St. Stephens College in Delhi. We missed our in-person meetings, phone calls became redundant, and we were no longer excited about being together. Finally, we broke up a year back".

"Every end is a new beginning, buddy! Let's walk back. It is getting late". Saesha turned around and headed in the direction of the hostel.

"Now it's your turn". Akshay was excited this time.

"I don't have any cute teenage romantic story like you; all I have is a complicated relationship". She looked back towards Akshay, spoke, and then continued walking.

"Ohh, come on. How old are you? 19 or 20, and you boast of being in a complicated relationship? Then you have not seen enough life. I am not kiddo; you are the real kiddo". Akshay walked faster towards her and uttered in credence. Saesha realised that he was not as dumb as she thought he was. Saesha replied, "Impressive", which boosted Akshay's confidence in talking to an heir of billions of dollars.

Meanwhile, Saesha received a phone call and had to leave for urgent project work. Saesha apologised for leaving him alone midway and bid goodbye to him. Akshay continued returning to his hostel room, reminiscing his conversations with her. He experienced a refresh in life after talking to her. Intelligent, extremely rich, and a great cook! A girl way out of his league. Then the thought stuck in his mind: they didn't exchange any phone number or contact details.

"What an idiot I am; how will I find her again on this campus"? Akshay wondered.

CHAPTER SIX

A PECK ON THE CHEEK

*A*kshay narrated his meetup with Saesha the following day and went to Abhinav to inquire about her whereabouts. Abhinav was unaware of a girl of this background but promised Akshay to inquire with Debora and his other friends and revert. He believed Abhinav's words as he had built a decent social network within the University.

Akshay continued attending classes and working on the project, but he couldn't focus so well as before. His mind wandered through the memories of Saesha and how he could meet her again. She was absent on all social media channels, including LinkedIn, and he was also not sure of her surname, which reduced the impact of his searches. With no other option, he continued to look around for Saesha in all gatherings, hostel mess, library, playground, gymnasium, cafeterias, and almost wherever he went.

Two days passed on. Akshay had no trace of Saesha. He also wondered what made him so curious about Saesha. Was it because she was rich? Maybe not, because she was fun; there are many such girls here, and she was neither extremely beautiful nor cute. She was another stranger he interacted with in Montreal. That's it. Akshay decided to move on and take life as it came. That afternoon, while debugging a code in the research lab, he received a call from an unknown number. Akshay picked up. "Hello, remember me"? It was Saesha on the other side.

"Hey, of course. How are you"? Akshay replied in gratitude.

"I am doing well; you tell me".

"How did you get my number"? Akshay became curious.

"Only boys know how to stalk? I thought you would contact me before I did". Akshay was thrilled to know that she was expecting to meet him again.

Akshay: "I tried but couldn't succeed. Never mind, when do we meet next"?

Saesha: "How about this evening? Listen, as a part of my course project, I need to visit a few foster care centres here, and I felt you would be a good companion".

Akshay: "Sure. I think I can make myself free for the evening. Text me the details".

Akshay was unsure of the idea of visiting foster care centres. Nevertheless, he decided to try it out. They met at the main entrance and onboarded a cab to the destination. Saesha had a DSLR and a tripod to cover the visit.

"Is this what you do as a part of your course"? Her massive preparation for the visit made Akshay pose this question.

"Not really; my subject is more theoretical. But, my project guide wanted this favour from me as a part of his personal commitment. So, I had to pool in some time for it. Otherwise, at this stage, we focus on covering the theory of the subject and specialise after graduation. It can be either a theoretical research study or fieldwork in the areas of developmental studies, agriculture, human resources, health welfare, etc".

Akshay: "Okay, have you decided about the specialisation"?

Saesha: "I think I will focus more on theoretical research, and later, I aspire to work for humanitarian organisations like the Red Cross, Amnesty International, etc".

Akshay: "Then who will take charge of your family business"?

Saesha: "Myself. I will do both in tandem and contribute a significant portion of the profits to human welfare activities".

Akshay: "You are unbelievable. Had I been in your place, I would have just travelled around the world. You don't understand how privileged you are in society".

Saesha: "Exactly, I understand that I am privileged, and hence, I feel I must serve the society or the underprivileged".

"Hmm, Interesting", Akshay replied. Within a few minutes, they reached the place. Akshay assisted in setting up the arrangements for the shoots. Saesha interacted with the inmates in a friendly way with the help of a prepared questionnaire she had. She also played games with them, offered gifts, and took videos and photographs. The inmates consisted primarily of older people who preferred a community stay with people of their age group and interests. Unlike India, their kids didn't force them to be there; many preferred to be there by choice. And in fact, some or many of them were financially stable and wanted to lead a simple retired life.

She wrapped up the session in a few hours and asked Akshay, "What's the plan now"?

"Let's head for dinner somewhere". Akshay was hungry.

"Cools, I will take you to my favourite place here, Pizzadelic Mont-Royal".

That night, Akshay was introduced to a wide variety of mouthwatering French pizzas in Montreal. In addition, they ordered a spicy Poulet Thai to satisfy Akshay's Indian spicy cravings and a Cinq Fromages (a French cheese dish), one of Saesha's favourite dishes, along with two glasses of red wine.

"Have you seen any Indian movies"? Akshay asked while sipping the red wine.

"Yeah, a couple of them. I think the last movie that I watched was 3 Idiots".

"3 Idiots was a blockbuster hit in many Indian languages. Do you speak Tamil"? Akshay asked.

"I can pick up basic Tamil. What about you? Two years of Madras life must have made you learn". Saesha had almost finished her pizza, while Akshay was only halfway through. She wiped off the cheese from her hands using a tissue and prepared to strike up a conversation.

"Not really. I can only converse in basic Tamil due to interactions with my Tamil friends there, but otherwise, being in a college within the city doesn't give you an incentive to learn Tamil. The campus comprises everything like a shopping mall, sports complexes, and movie theatre, so we are almost self-sufficient. Also, some events or the other would always be happening inside the campus to keep us entertained. For example, I became a fan of professional dramas after joining college, and my passion for movies escalated. And listen, there is a movie you should watch in Tamil; it is titled 'Kannathil Muthamittal,' which means 'a peck on the cheek' in Tamil".

"Interesting, but why do you suggest this movie to me"? Saesha was curious.

"It is a 2002 Tamil movie that I recently watched and is directed by one of the best Indian directors, Mani Ratnam. I suggest the film to you primarily because of its plot. It speaks about the Sri Lankan riots and is essentially the story of a 10-year-old girl traveling to Sri Lanka searching for her mother and her foster parents".

Saesha didn't appreciate the plot much; she looked disturbed once Akshay completed it.

"Why, what happened? Is the plot not interesting to you"? Akshay got doubtful of his movie suggestion.

"Not at all; I expected you would suggest a fun movie to me; this looks pretty serious". Saesha arose from her thoughts.

"Yeah, a bit, but I feel it is worth watching. Many aspects of filmmaking, like screenplay, dialogues, music, performances, cinematography, and direction, have fallen into place beautifully. Moreover, I was deeply excited by the idea of adopting a girl child or, in the worst-case, contributing towards the education and health of orphan children once I start earning. I mean, the movie had a powerful impact on my outlook on life. Check it out if you get time". Akshay explained his rationale for suggesting the movie.

"Sure, boss! I will do that. Let's head back to campus". Saesha noticed Akshay had also finished his meal, and they were ready to leave.

"Yeah, sure. I will book a cab". Akshay picked up his phone to book a return journey. Saesha didn't speak much inside the cab; she appeared lost in thoughts, maybe because they had a tiring day. Finally, after a long gap of silence, Saesha proposed a plan.

"How about we plan a bucket list of activities to be done in Montreal together and complete them one by one before we head back to our home universities? You would also be benefitted as I can be a valuable free guide and buddy".

"Aren't you also new to this country"? He judged her overconfidence.

"But I am smarter". She agreed to Akshay's judgment.

"Definitely. You are indeed smarter, one of the smartest I have seen," Akshay replied.

After reaching campus and before dispersing back to their respective rooms, Akshay asked about the next catchup plan. "I am occupied for the next two days with my project work.

How about we catch up on this Friday evening? We can go out somewhere, and I will have a surprise for you". She confidently smirked, to which he agreed immediately.

"Okay, bye. Take care; Debora is my room neighbour; that's how I got your contact number". Saesha said this and walked away naturally without waiting for Akshay's response.

Akshay cursed Abhinav for being hopeless in life. He could only gaze at Saesha till she walked away from his sight. The teenage girl had opened another chapter of herself tonight. Kindness and compassionate attitude while maintaining consistency in her intelligent thoughts. Akshay had time till Friday to think of the surprise she had in store for him.

CHAPTER SEVEN

WITHIN THE HAND'S REACH

"*M*eet you in front of the central library at 9 pm, be dressed in smart casuals. Got a plan for the night"! Saesha texted Akshay on Friday evening.

Akshay wore blue denim and a white shirt and waited for Saesha in front of the library on time. She joined in a few minutes, wearing a beautiful red gown and a shiny diamond necklace. "You look beautiful". Akshay couldn't stop expressing himself. She smiled and thanked him.

"Come, let's go". She advanced her steps. Akshay followed, further admiring her sense of style and attitude. "Where are we heading to"? Akshay couldn't wait any longer. "Have you heard of the notorious nightclub, Stereo Club, in Montreal"? Akshay replied a No to Saesha's informative question.

"It is one of the most sought-after party places in Montreal, where you can sing, dance, drink, and may experiment more". She explained further.

"Are we going there now"? Akshay was surprised. She nodded with a lot of excitement.

"Why did you mention notorious"? Akshay wondered.

"It is infamous for the general availability of the drug GHB that is often used as a date rape drug during the party. But never mind, it is a safe place. It's only a matter of choice to stay safe there. It is pretty known for its famous sound system and possession of loyal followers".

"Hmm, Okay. The issue is that I am not a party person but sceptical about that". Akshay expressed his concern.

"Okay, I will give it a shot this time. And I am sure this is the party you would have never seen". Saesha was confident.

The stereo nightclub in the Quebec province featured horse and techno music primarily on weekends. They entered the club after being closely scanned by three six-foot-tall bouncers at the entrance who looked spine-chilling. It appeared they were a bit early for the party, as the arena was getting filled. The nightclub had a two-floor configuration, with the upper constituting the after-hours portion for the nightlife parties and the lower floor for a smaller nightclub that runs throughout the day. The lower floor was more silent than the upper floor, where the techno DJ had already started his performance. Akshay noticed bar counters and many beers, wines, and cocktails served to the audience. The crowd appeared younger and premium. Saesha dragged Akshay to the drinks counter to kickstart the party. The bartender offered a craft beer variant as Saesha instructed.

"Cheers to the special night", Saesha said, raising her beer glass for Akshay.

Akshay found the taste pretty different, smooth and bitter-free, unlike the traditional Kingfisher beer he had tasted in India. Later they ventured into other options like Belvedre, Cognac, and Bombay Sapphire. This deadly trio set the mood for the stage, and both started swooning to the enrapturing music. Meanwhile, they met another friend of Saesha from her college who introduced them to a strange white powder. Saesha verified the nature of the drug, and she was comforted by her friend that it was a mild one. Both of them snorted the drug through a white pipe and re-entered the party with more vigour. Akshay appreciated the scintillating colours, the musical vibrations, the trance crowd, and Saesha's dance moves like never before.

After half an hour on the dance floor, Akshay decided to take a break and moved to a quieter corner. He watched Saesha, wholly absorbed in the vibrant and loud atmosphere there. 'She truly knows how to live in the moment,' he thought to himself, closing his eyes for a few minutes as he wandered through his thoughts. When he opened his eyes, Saesha was nowhere to be seen in the crowd. He searched for her on both floors, near the bar counter, and even in the washrooms, but she was nowhere to be found. Feeling anxious and frustrated, Akshay waited at the same spot, hoping she would return, but she didn't. As the party continued to pulse with energy, Akshay grew increasingly uneasy. He decided to step outside and found himself walking through the quiet, empty streets of Quebec. A few meters away from the nightclub, he spotted someone sitting alone on a red bench. It was Saesha, her back to him, lost in her thoughts.

"Where were you? I was searching…" Akshay raised his voice before he was interrupted by a tight hug from Saesha, who was waking up from the bench.

"What happened, Saesha? Anything went wrong at the party. I am sorry, I was sloshed for a while". Saesha loosened the hug and turned around. Akshay noticed that she was crying in her half sense. "What happened? Tell me"? Akshay raised his voice again

"I am sorry, I got a bit emotional. Today is my Birthday, my 20th Birthday". She told.

"Damn! You didn't tell me. Happy Birthday, girl"! Saesha didn't reply. She had tears in her eyes.

"How can she cry so elegantly"? Akshay inappropriately wondered.

"Do you remember, Akshay, that you identified me as an Indian in our first meeting? Some judge me to be Pakistani, a few to be Spanish, and some mistake me to be Italian because of my accent. Today is the day I judge this mixed identity myself. Today is a good day because, on this date, my parents adopted me from an orphanage in Florence fifteen years back, and it is a bad day because I get reminded of my true self, and I feel incredibly lonely in this vast world".

Akshay pinched his hand multiple times to have a reality check, and he everytime succeeded.

"I was not born to my parents, who migrated from Sri Lanka. They are my foster parents, who were kind enough to offer me a blessed life. I was not born privileged; they chose me to be one". Saesha continued.

Akshay found himself at a loss for words as he watched Saesha, tears streaming down her face. The girl who smiled the most elegantly also owned the most beautiful tears. Just three weeks ago, he had believed that the world was vast, and that modern life was defined by individualism. Now, as he sat beside her on the bench, he realized that perhaps the world didn't always have to be vast and complicated; it could be as simple and small as this moment shared on the bench.

Saesha wiped away her tears and glanced around, her eyes falling upon a vibrant, lush green grasshopper hopping over the street plants. Enthralled by the sight, she extended her hand, and the grasshopper hopped onto her palm. She gently stroked its back, a smile slowly returning to her face.

Watching this scene unfold, Akshay marvelled at how quickly the grasshopper had brought a smile to Saesha's tear-streaked face. Akshay, who oversaw the entire scene, wished in his mind.

"If I were the hopper, if I were the hopper on her palm, if I were the hopper on her palm forever".

CHAPTER EIGHT

BEFORE SUNRISE

"*W*hat belongs to you today, belonged to someone yesterday and will be someone else's tomorrow".

"My grandmother narrated this verse to me as a kid, and it still sticks in my mind. I am not sure if that helps you. But if you think about it, you have everything in life now: professional education, good health, amazing friends, immense wealth, lovely parents, and a human mentality to give back to society. How many in the world are created by the almighty so meticulously? You are a gem of a person"! Finally, Akshay tried his best to console Saesha.

"I know, right? But at times, the memories muddle ineptly, and every year on this day, it reaches the pinnacle of incertitude. Who are my real parents? Are they alive somewhere? What are their nationalities? What language do they speak? Why did they leave me at a young age? Can any mother do that to their child? Or did they lose me somewhere and are still searching for me? In that case, how can I get back to them? When your mind unravels through such thoughts, it is traumatic, and you lose your sanity. I don't want to be a rebellious teenager, but at times, being one gives me the peace of mind I crave. In addition, it grants a distinctive identity where I negate all the social norms existing in society". Saesha took another pause.

"Saesha, I understand what you are saying. It's just a phase, and this shall also pass. Believe in yourself and translate with the flow".

"I am not sure how long it will take for me to be at peace with this distorted identity.

Anyway, talking to you today makes me feel better. Thanks, Akshay"! Saesha walked towards a public washroom nearby to clear her face of the tears. Akshay waited outside. She returned in a few minutes, and they continued walking along the windless roads.

"How are you feeling now"? Akshay asked.

"What came and went through, the most in my life were friends. It was through meaningful companionships that I overcame my loneliness. I shared my problems, joy, excitement, sorrow, agony, successes, and failures. I valued them and endeavoured to keep them close and not lose them. But after a certain point, we all parted in our ways. What I believed to be forever was an interim arrangement. This makes me vulnerable in life; I wonder if I am destined to be alone. Do you know what my biggest fear in life is? Losing my dear ones"!

Akshay: "That's the case with most of us in our generation. I am also not in touch with many of my childhood friends, whom I thought would be my amigos for life. That's all life is about. Variety is life's spice; hence, we embrace change with open hands".

Saesha: "It's more complicated than what I narrated. Certain things can be understood only if you experience them, and it is hard to explain them through words. Or wait, let me give you an anecdote from my childhood. Following my adoption, adjusting to a new house with unfamiliar faces, rooms, food, and furniture proved to be a daunting task. Everything seemed luxurious yet distant. The only connection I found was with an orange Persian cat named Simba, who was raised in the house. Our bond was immediate, but tragedy struck when a neighbourhood dog killed her within a few months. Overwhelmed with grief, I lost control. In anger and desperation, I took a can of kerosene, approached the dog, poured a few drops on its tail, and ignited it with a matchstick I carried".

Akshay's mouth was wide open. "In what trance stage are you in"? Akshay questioned.

"A neighbour came to the dog's rescue, and fortunately, he was saved. Later, I was taken to a medical hospital checkup and had to undergo a few Post Traumatic Stress Disorder medications and treatment for a few months. I don't know if all that helped, but over a period, I came back to life". Saesha continued.

Akshay: "It's the deadly trio and the white powder in action now, my trance girl! Let's get back to campus. You will feel much better then".

Saesha: "I wanted to show you around this part of the province; I had one more surprise".

Akshay: "I appreciate your enthusiasm, Saesha. But I think you certainly need rest. So, I am booking a cab to campus".

Saesha: "Okay, your choice".

Saesha and Akshay took a cab back, resting comfortably on Akshay's shoulders and drifting into a peaceful nap. Akshay ensured the windows were open to let in the cool night air, though the Uber driver seemed indifferent to their comfort. Upon reaching Saesha's place, Akshay gently helped her to her room and laid her down on the bed, tucking her in with a cosy bedsheet.

As Akshay looked around, he noticed that Saesha's room reflected her personality—well-organised, with carefully chosen artefacts, paintings, and handicrafts adorning the walls and window frames. Lost in the beauty of her room, Akshay was surprised when Saesha reached out and held his hand, pleading softly, "Don't leave me alone tonight; stay, make me feel special".

Akshay gladly joined her under the covers, which enveloped them in warmth. He ran his fingers through her hair, tracing the contours of her ears, nose, and lips, each touch igniting a gentle spark between them. Saesha playfully nibbled on his fingers, and as Akshay moved to pull away, she drew closer, their lips almost touching. At that moment, Akshay wished for the night to stretch on endlessly, but...

"Hey!! Morning! How did it feel last night"? Saesha woke up Akshay around 5 am. "It was a roller coaster ride, an eventful night, but thanks to the happy ending"! Akshay giggled.

"I have one more surprise pending for you! Wake up"! Saesha pulled Akshay's hands out of bed. "That's too much, Saesha; please surprise me later". Akshay was tired, physically and mentally.

Saesha occupied the chair in front of Akshay and emoted greater displeasure. Finally, Akshay woke up from the bed and asked. "Okay, where are we going"?

"Are you scared of me"? She was not expecting Akshay to agree that easily. "Maybe not of you, but of some of your expressions". He replied, rubbing his tired eyes.

Saesha grinned to ease the situation and replied, "Come, just hold my hands and hike for ten minutes".

They were heading to Mont-Royal through the inner roads of the University. Mont-Royal is a small rock mountain located in Montreal, which can be accessed easily through the internal streets of Montreal University. Situated between the Laurentians and the Appalachian Mountains, Montreal drew its name from Mont-Royal, part of the Monteregian hills. One of Montreal's most sought-after tourist attractions is a profound extension of a vastly eroded ancient complex of volcanos. The Mont-Royal viewpoint stands close to two hundred meters above the city centre, and the area around it acts as the green lungs for Montreal downtown. A magnificent vista of the fifty-one km length of the city centre and Saint Lawrence River awaits at the summit. If you are lucky and the sky is clear, the view might extend to the Adirondack Mountains in the United States of America.

They reached the viewpoint in the next few minutes. Around thirty-plus people were eagerly waiting to witness the sunrise and exchanged smiles with each other. The sun rose gently, and Akshay astonishingly observed how each ray touched every building with its warm, charming lights. The view mesmerised him, and Akshay realised that if not for Saesha, he would have missed this experience in Montreal. He looked at her and thanked her for existing as a beautiful soul. Akshay noticed Saesha was highly delighted and contented, which was the opposite of the previous night. He wished to believe that he also had a handful of contributions towards her happiness.

Meanwhile, Saesha pointed Akshay towards a sloppy land on the right and asked, "Can you guess what that area is"?

"It looks like a cemetery", Akshay answered.

"Yeah, it is. An ancient one, though. This country has witnessed immigration for centuries, and that land houses the graveyard of the early settlers from different parts of the world and diverse ethnicities. Whenever I see such cemeteries, I wonder if my parents also rest there"?

Akshay went closer to the cemetery and read the death year written on one tomb, which was mentioned as 1875. "Yeah, this indeed looks like your father's". He replied sarcastically with an evil smile.

Saesha restlessly looked around. A long, sharp wooden stick was lying nearby. She grabbed the rod and raised it against Akshay's shoulders. Akshay ran down the hill at his maximum throttle in anticipation of being hit while Saesha followed him with an all-encompassing vigour.

CHAPTER NINE

EMBRACE YOUR DESIRE

With its modernity and rich history, Montreal exudes an old-school European elegance that sets it apart. The city offers a blend of contemporary allure and a deep-rooted past, evident in its Mont-Royal viewpoints and charming Old Montreal restaurants. These eateries offer diverse cuisines and a stunning rooftop view for a memorable dining experience. Montreal's culinary reputation precedes it, boasting a legendary scene with many restaurants, cafes, and bistros serving tantalising dishes. From classic French delicacies to innovative fusion creations, Montreal's food scene mirrors its status as a culinary capital.

As Summer arrives in Montreal, the city transforms into a playground of vibrant life and celebration. Residents emerge to revel in the season, embracing the plentiful arts and entertainment offerings. World-class museums, galleries, and theatres showcase the talents of local and international artists. At the same time, the city's music scene thrives with venues ranging from cosy jazz clubs to grand concert halls, hosting a diverse range of performances.

For Montrealers, the warmer months from June to September are synonymous with festivals, culinary delights, and outdoor adventures.

Akshay and Saesha were occupied with their academic commitments for the next few days and met up in the middle of their hectic schedules within the campus, as exploring Montreal was not feasible. Abhinav, Debora, and the other batchmates also hosted a few house parties, which they attended. These informal drinking and gaming sessions reminded Akshay of his hostel terrace parties. In one such party, Akshay reminded Saesha of the activities they had to cover in Montreal in the next three weeks before returning to their respective home colleges. The thought of leaving Montreal would make Akshay extremely anxious. He had reached a situation where he couldn't spend a day without meeting Saesha. He always wondered if that was the same with her. Despite being together for weeks, Saesha remained a mystery to him; she constituted many emotions that were hard to comprehend.

"What are the remaining places on the bucket list"? Saesha enquired.

"Montreal cycle rally, Tango dance workshop, Montreal Jazz festival, Montreal International Fireworks Competition, Annual Summer Arts Festival, Place de arts, Little Italy, 360-degree view of Montreal from Place Ville Marie Observatory, and the visit to the adult entertainment clubs". Akshay blushed.

"Okay, what shall we do first"? Saesha raised the question to everyone.

"Do you want an honest or a diplomatic answer"? Akshay woke up from his seat and answered

Saesha thought for a while, smiled, and replied, "Honest".

"Okay, Cabaret Kingdom is Montreal's most-rated adult entertainment club. Shall we go this Friday"? Akshay was crystal clear on his priority.

"Done". Saesha, though brought up in Europe, has not been to one yet, and she was also exhilarated about the idea and wanted to explore the options in Montreal. Saesha was also excited.

"There is an Airbnb experience booking for the Tango workshop in the third week of every month; we should try it out", Debora suggested.

"Cools. I guess we have a sorted plan then. We can participate in the Tango dance workshop on the third weekend of the month, and the Montreal cycle rally is scheduled for the last week, a few days before we leave. For the rest of the places, we will try to sandwich between these dates and finish off. So, let's try to frontload our academic work to pool in enough time for fun. Sounds good"? Abhinav, Akshay, and Debora agreed to Saesha's plan.

The Tango was a partner and social dance with Latin American origins predominant in the European countries and their established colonies. With an inherent French culture, Montreal constituted many tango workshops that were attended in pairs. The Montreal Cycle Rally is Canada's most famous city cycle rally, which happens every Summer. During that day, the entire city goes to a standstill as all the city inhabitants find time to participate in this rally and take a complete tour of the city. The Montreal Fireworks competition explodes pretty colours all over the Montreal city skyline perfectly. Attendees can pay to sit at the front and centre, but that's primarily the tourists; the locals prefer to take a backseat. There are also secret sweet spots wherein you can have fun with groups of travellers through music, drinks, and bonfires. Montreal, known for its top-notch music scene, hosts the world-famous jazz festival during Summer, starting at the end of June every year. But the festival is not just limited to big players and big bucks; you can also enjoy equally talented local artists who sing across genres for free during the day hours.

With this tentative plan, they decided to remain in this beautiful city for the next few weeks. But do you know what the best way to make God laugh is? Make plans!

As a part of her project requirement, Saesha was asked to relocate to Toronto for the next ten days. As a result, she had to conduct development studies fieldwork by collaborating with the local daily, The Toronto Citizen. Akshay was devastated to know that Saesha would leave in two days. Saesha noticed his disappointment, which was very expressive in his eyes.

"We will finish off all the places in the bucket list items after I come back. It's my word. Don't worry, Akshay".

Akshay was not worried about visiting all the places; he was more concerned about the presence of Saesha around him. He knew their paths would diverge by this month-end, wherein life would take different turns for both of them, and they would never meet again. Nonetheless, he didn't want to lose the valuable ten days he possesses now.

The next day, Saesha texted Akshay that she would leave the airport by 5 p.m. and wanted to meet him for evening tea. Akshay agreed. Saesha completed packing, prebooked a cab, and waited for Akshay at 4:30 p.m. in the cafeteria. Unfortunately, contrary to his punctuality nature, Akshay didn't arrive on time. A disappointed Saesha tried calling him.

"I am so sorry, Saesha; I will be there in ten minutes". But Akshay didn't turn up as promised. Saesha, with extreme disappointment, walked toward the cab close to 5 p.m. Akshay was waiting there.

"You are a loser"! Saesha cursed Akshay and opened the car trunk to keep her luggage in.

"Whose luggage is this"? Saesha wondered. Akshay replied, "Mine", and entered the cab.

"Akshay, don't tell me you are coming with me to Toronto". She screamed, "Why not"? Akshay replied with a graceful smile after occupying the cab backseat. "What about your project then"? Saesha bent down and asked Akshay, who was already settled inside the cab.

"I am an engineer, essentially a problem solver. So, don't worry about it; come, let's leave, or we will be delayed at the airport". He confidently replied. A speechless but delighted Saesha occupied the seat and asked the driver to start the journey to the airport.

"It's unbelievable, Akshay. How did you convince your project guide"? She was still in her astonishment.

"I am working on a coding assignment now; all I need is a good laptop, a stable internet connection, and a comfortable workplace.

Fortunately, my project guide is unavailable on campus until this month, and we interact through Skype calls. Then, my next and last aim was to convince the project buddy of the plan of working remotely for the next ten days".

"How did you do that"? She raised her curiosity. Akshay smiled confidently and recollected his interaction with the project buddy, James Taylor.

* * *

"What's the plan for the next ten days"? His project guide, Mr Taylor, asked Akshay the reason for his leave.

"A friend, another exchange student from Brussels, is heading to Toronto for research work. I thought we would explore the city together. I have not seen enough of Canada apart from Montreal". Akshay replied cautiously.

"Okay, what's her name"?

"Her name is Saesha". Akshay blushed and replied.

"Is that an Indian name? What does it mean"? Akshay apologised and replied to Mr Taylor that he was unaware of the meaning of the name.

"Google says the meaning is "desire". Mr Taylor quickly searched for the meaning of "Saesha's name" on Google.

"Okay, go ahead. But don't forget to send me daily updates and attend the check-in regularly. Who conducted the advanced mass transfer session for you"? He warned Akshay and posed another question.

"Madam Susanne", Akshay replied.

"Six years back, my wife and I were exchange students at the University. She was from Bulgaria, and I was a native of Vancouver. She is your Madam Susanne. Go buddy, go embrace your desire"! Mr. Taylor pushed Akshay outside of his room.

* * *

"Tell me, Akshay, how did you convince your buddy"? Saesha repeated her question as Akshay stood in silence for a while.

"It was not necessary to convince him; he just advised me to go and embrace my desire".

CHAPTER TEN

CELEBRATION OF LIFE

The skyscraper city of Canada, Toronto, is known for its high-rise buildings, particularly the tallest free-standing structure in the Western Hemisphere, the CN Tower. The iconic CN Tower, once the tallest free-standing structure in the world, dominates the skyline, offering panoramic views of the city and beyond. Located on the shores of Lake Ontario, Toronto's waterfront is a hub of activity, with parks, beaches, and waterfront trails offering stunning views of the lake and the city skyline. The Toronto Islands, just a short ferry ride away, provide a peaceful escape from the hustle and bustle of the city, with beaches, bike paths, and quaint cottages adding to the charm. Apart from the concrete structures, it is famous for its delicious street meat, hot dogs, and sausage. A dish of French fries and cheese curds topped with a brown gravy called Poutine is a must-try in Toronto. It has been hailed "Canada's national dish", and many annual poutine celebrations occur in various parts of the city.

However, perhaps the most notable is Toronto's welcoming spirit and sense of community. The city's residents, hailing from all corners of the globe, come together to celebrate their diversity through festivals, events, and cultural activities, creating a vibrant and inclusive atmosphere that defines Toronto as a truly global city.

Akshay and Saesha landed in Toronto late at night. The booked hotel was twenty minutes away from the city.

"How about we use the city metro to reach the hotel? It seems the hotel is closer to the metro station". Akshay was keen on traveling on the trains, as he was tired of the continuous luxurious cab travels.

"Are you sure"? Saesha cross-checked. "Yeah, we also have less luggage with us. I think we can manage". He reaffirmed his decision, and Saesha agreed with the idea. They were onboarded to the metro train, which was sparsely populated.

Saesha: "What's your plan for the day, Akshay? I will have to report at the news' daily office".

Akshay: "Yeah, that's fine. I will work from the hotel room or lobby".

Saesha: "Okay, if I get free in the daytime, I will ping you; you also do the same".

Akshay: "Sure, aren't you excited about this Toronto trip"?

Saesha: "Yeah, definitely".

Akshay: "I hope I didn't invade your privacy by tagging along with you".

Saesha laughed and replied, "Now I don't have any other choice". Akshay was unsure if she was joking or meant it. Saesha occupied the seat opposite Akshay in the compartment. She shifted position and took the seat beside Akshay.

"What was the movie's name, Kannathil Muthamitttal (Peck on the cheek)"? She moved closer to Akshay's face and kissed on his cheek. "Yes". His face blossomed.

The initial Toronto days were lukewarm. Akshay and Saesha met for lunches, evening walks, and snacks if their schedules permitted. On a night when both got free early in the evening, they decided to explore the downtown. They wandered through the city lights, explored the local food streets, went window shopping, and listened to fantastic street musical performances. The outdoor Toronto musicians who make the soundscape a better place are termed buskers. Sometimes, it can be solo performances like the famous Jeff Burke, who plays Bassoon and Theremin and creates a larger-than-life sound in the bustling Bloor station. Or band performances of the likes of the six-piece funk band Turbo Street Funk, the regular crowd-pleasers at Toronto's Scotiabank Buskers Fest every year.

Akshay and Saesha noticed a band performance close to the city centre. They opted to listen to them with the crowd, who were engrossed in the music or busy dancing to the tunes. The atmosphere induced abundant positivity in them. "Western life is pretty simple, right"? Akshay posted this inner doubt to Saesha; she wondered why he felt so all of a sudden.

"In India, people hardly enjoy themselves so freely in public. Look at that couple; they must be in their middle ages, yet they don't care what society thinks of them; they dance beautifully with their hearts. At times, I feel that the family culture in India is a burden; there are many stakeholders to be managed, and you don't get to live your own life. In most cases, you end up living for others". Akshay explained. Saesha thought for a while and asked Akshay to look at an old uncle standing on one of the street corners

"Yeah, not just him; many companionless people are in the crowd". Akshay almost guessed where she was heading to.

"Living in Western society has its advantages and disadvantages. I am not denying that they are not enjoying the performance by staying alone; some might have preferred to live isolated. But I am certain some might be going through their worst times. Years of loneliness and solitary living might have destroyed their mental health. In fact, I have closely known many such people in my life. Given a scenario, I believe having your people as a fallback option is good. Dealing with loneliness is any day worse than managing your stakeholders. The grass is always greener on the other side, Akshay"!

"Yeah, maybe that's true. I am new to this way of living and should take time to absorb it into the system completely". Akshay sensed it to be a very subjective and broad topic that may not conclude anything at the end of the discussion.

Toronto days and life continued. The weekend has finally arrived, and they decided to visit an adult entertainment club on Friday night. The Montreal bucket list item was shifted to Toronto for two reasons. First, the Montreal days were already lowered, and second, the Zanzibar Tavern Club in Toronto appeared to be more famous and entertaining than the options in Montreal. The Zanzibar Tavern, the major local landmark of the renowned downtown street Yonge Street Strip, is one of the oldest nightclubs in Toronto, which recently celebrated its golden jubilee. In numerous Hollywood films, this place has appeared, the most famous citing in the 2008 Marvel superhero film, The Incredible Hulk. This place is christened as the "Psychedelic Avenue" of the Yonge Street strip and is known for its environment filled with stroboscopic lights, mannequins, and closed-circuit cameras that take photos of the dance floor and project them on the wall.

After being scanned by the bouncers, they entered the club, who were less majestic than the ones spotted in Montreal. They passed through a long pathway before reaching the main arena. The main hall consisted of two levels in addition to the central stage where the dance performances occur. The primary level was accessible to everyone, while the second level, close to the stage, required you to pay an entrance fee. Akshay and Saesha decided to occupy a seat in the primary arena. The area had a crowded mix skewed towards the women. "What's your plan, Akshay"? Saesha asked.

Akshay: "I have no idea. You should tell me".

"Choose a stripper from the crowd, converse for a while, and then go for a lap dance. That's the bare minimum you should do; we can plan the rest accordingly". Saesha giggled.

Akshay: "Then what will you do"?

Saesha: "I will do the same or be your wingman for the night. I will go and get you a drink now".

She left the place, and Akshay looked around. So many of the strippers were extraordinarily gorgeous and reminded him of the supermodels seen in movies or TV series. The central stage performance was also beautifully orchestrated; someone pats him from behind. Akshay looked around. There was none. He immediately shifted to his original posture. In a white two-piece dress, the girl he found the most attractive among the strippers was sitting opposite where Saesha sat.

Girl: "Hey, I am Elizabeth, you can call me Liza".

Akshay: "Hi Liza, I am Akshay".

Liza: "Who was the girl with you, your girlfriend"?

This question perplexed him. Akshay wondered if he would be happy to reply with a yes to the question. However, he was confused about a Yes; hence, he answered a No.

Akshay: "No, she is my friend. We are studying at the University of Montreal".

Liza: "What brings you to Toronto, then"?

Akshay: "So, my friend's name is Saesha. She has to be here in Toronto for ten days as a part of her course project, and that's why we are here".

Liza: "Okay, so are you guys part of the same project"?

Akshay: "No, I am sorry. I am an engineering student, and she is from the sociology department. We are here on an exchange term. My home university is IIT Madras in India, and she is from the Brussels School of Economics and Management".

Liza: "Then, what are you doing here in Toronto, honey"?

Akshay: "I am working remotely on my laptop".

Liza: "Interesting"!

Meanwhile, Saesha returned with drinks. She noticed Akshay had picked up a girl, offered him the drink, and replied. "I will join you guys in a while". She smiled at both.

Liza: "Hi Saesha, I am Liza".

Saesha: "Hey! How do you know my name"?

Liza: "Akshay just spoke about you".

Saesha: "Hey! That's nice of you, Akshay".

"I shouldn't be the topic of your conversations", Saesha murmured to his ears and left. Liza and Akshay both smiled at each other.

"So, tell me about you". Akshay spoke with confidence.

Liza: "I am also a student doing my MPhil in theology and working as a part-time employee with this club".

"I am sorry to ask this. M-Phil in Theology and a part-time profession in an adult entertainment club, what an irony"? Akshay was surprised to know that she is pursuing a post-graduation degree.

Liza: "Never, God is love, and love is God".

Both laughed at her reply.

Akshay: "Are these the cases with all the girls working in this club"?

Liza: "Not really; some of us are part-time, some are full-time, and we come from varying backgrounds. However, a common thing would be that we would have a unique story to tell".

Akshay and Liza continued their conversations. Saesha watched them while attending the dance performances on the central stage. Saesha expected Akshay to upgrade himself from discussions, but she was disappointed. Liza stood from the chair, kissed Akshay on the cheek, and spoke, "Take care, Akshay; I need to leave now. Also, Akshay, you are in love"!

"Hey! What happened"? Saesha rushed to Akshay and asked.

Akshay: "Nothing; we spoke for a while, and she left me".

Saesha: "That's it"?

Akshay: "Yeah, that's it".

Saesha: "Never mind. Let's look for another girl".

Akshay: "No. Let's finish the drink and leave the place".

Saesha: "Come on, Akshay, you can't be a party pooper".

Akshay agreed to stay half-heartedly. They had more drinks, smokes, and dance performances. There was substantial hard work behind the performances in choreography, costume, themes, and performers. An hour later, they exited the club and walked through the streets. It was close to 2:30 am, and they couldn't find any public transport to get to the hotel. "Akshay, are you falling in love with me"? She raised a query. "I don't know; right now, Liza told me I was in love before the kiss. How could she tell that"? Akshay smiled at her question and replied.

Saesha: "Interesting. So, I will tell you my perspective about love, the love between two people or rather between two entities. Firstly, I feel it is heavily exaggerated through art, literature, and movies. What you see in real life is different from the reels. People get into relationships out of convenience and leave them apart when they find a better, more convenient choice. Isn't that ridiculous? For example, consider my parents' case; I don't think they are in love anymore".

Akshay: "Why do you think so"?

Saesha: "They had a legendary love story, starting from their elopement from Sri Lanka to Europe during the Sri Lankan civil war days. They continued to be in love, worked hard together, and earned a fortune. But I don't find them excited about living and growing together these days. They are rarely seen together, and during their meeting, it is all business that they speak about. So now, where has the love gone"?

Akshay's interest in the conversations increased.

"After a lot of brainstorming, I decided to believe that life is all about cherishing the moments and staying away from any commitments, which may be an attached detachment way of living. To live life is a rarity these days; most people just exist. I could be wrong; I might fall in love at one point in the future. When that happens, I will probably also start believing in it. But that moment has not come yet to me".

"You could have simply told me that you don't have any feelings towards me. I wouldn't have been hurt". Akshay laughed and then spoke.

"I meant it, Akshay; each word I spoke; it was not diplomacy". Saesha reacted in a severe tone.

Akshay: "Right. I was also pretty clear from day one of our meetings until Liza confused me. Since we have spoken about it, it's all cleared again".

Akshay paused and asked, "So, what's the definition of love in your opinion"?

"Tricky question, Akshay. I think the best comment I can pass on is this. It's an unconstrained, unrestricted, and unconditional emotion where you become a better human every day. When you love and are loved, you tend to be kind and compassionate; you appreciate nature, rain, sunsets, and thunder more. It's the most beautiful prayer in the world".

"You are overthinking"! Akshay warned her. "Maybe, but if we don't overthink at this age, then what's the fun? It's better to be confused now than to be ignorant. I think our conversations are getting serious". Saesha raised a concern, to which Akshay agreed.

"Tell me, Akshay, what do you want to do with your life"? She tried to change the topic.

Akshay: "I believe the plan was to stop serious conversations".

"Welcome, only cranky answers". Saesha laughed and corrected herself. "I can't think of any cranky reply, but now I feel I have only one answer to this question since I thought about it. Decades later, if I need to speak about my life, I should have a fairytale to narrate, not a normal one". Akshay thought for a while and replied.

Saesha: "What do you mean by a 'normal life'"?

Akshay: "By normal life, I mean the kind of life my parents' generation had. They had a sacrificing life, where they toiled in their government office for thirty-plus years, earned a decent salary, ate decent food, and then enjoyed the little happiness in life through a normal routine. I am not sure if you will be able to relate to it".

Saesha: "That sounds great to me. It looks like a fairy tale life. Life is otherwise pretty unfair"!

Akshay: "Yeah, I agree. I think my narration got messed up badly. After the narration, I also wondered what was wrong with this normal lifestyle".

Both burst into laughter.

Saesha: "Now we know who is confused. However, I believe all these discussions add perspective and colours to life. We should be proud of ourselves".

Akshay: "Now, no more serious discussions. I am serious"!

Saesha: "Yes, and for that, we need more drinks. Let's check out the nearest pub and walk in that direction".

Akshay and Saesha traversed into the unending long nights. Every day, the Toronto nights competed with the teenage pair to be more restless, young, and vibrant, but the success always rested with the high-spirited juvenile pair. Akshay's fairytale story had already begun!

When life calls for a celebration, isn't it a fairytale already?

CHAPTER ELEVEN

CHEERS TO MONTREAL

One day later, they flew back to Montreal. With exactly ten days remaining before their return to their home colleges, Akshay and Saesha had a list of pending tasks to complete. They needed to finalize their research reports, shop for their families in Canada, visit the remaining places in Montreal, and prepare themselves mentally and physically for the return journey. Akshay wanted souvenirs for his nephews and nieces, such as cosy knitted jackets, sweaters, and dream catchers. On the other hand, Saesha planned to take home some unique Canadian maple syrup.

The Montreal bucket list had narrowed to two items: attending the rescheduled tango dance workshop and participating in the Montreal City Cycle rally. The tango workshop, held in the famous Verdun Greenhouse zone, was a ninety-minute session that began with a fascinating history lesson over a glass of wine. Akshay, Saesha, and another Australian couple were the only attendees, as Abhinav and Debora had to miss out. The instructor explained that tango originated in the latter half of the nineteenth century along the border between Argentina and Uruguay, blending Uruguayan Candombe, Spanish-Cuban Habanera, and Argentinean Milonga music and dance forms.

After the theory session, the instructor taught some basic steps, which Akshay and Saesha, both new to the dance world, quickly picked up. They then had the opportunity to experiment with their steps with different partners under the instructor's guidance. It was a fun and engaging night for both, and Akshay discovered a newfound interest in dance and music, sparking a desire to explore more in the future.

The final event of their Montreal adventure was the cycle rally, in which Akshay, Saesha, Abhinav, and Debora enthusiastically participated. The eleven-kilometre rally was one of Montreal's most exhilarating experiences, even though they didn't come close to winning. The one-hour city ride took them through the bustling streets, where they witnessed a sea of people enjoying the event with their loved ones. The city was adorned with well-defined pathways, colourful billboards, informative signboards, inviting tents, and lively recreation zones, adding to the festive atmosphere.

On Akshay's final night in Montreal, the reality of their imminent departures sank in. With an early morning flight to Chennai, he would soon bid farewell to the city he had grown to love. Saesha was preparing for her journey to Florence later that day. Abhinav had plans to fly to Dubai in the afternoon to spend time with his cousins.

As they contemplated their departures, Abhinav and Saesha decided to book a cab together to the airport, sharing a final moment of camaraderie before parting ways. Akshay, however, would make his way to the airport alone, each step a reminder of the memories and friendships forged during their time in Montreal.

As a farewell to the three leaving students, Debora and her friends arranged a mini house party in her room. Unlike the previous parties, it was simple, with minimal lights and decorations but great drinks and smokes. Three of them completed all their packing and assembled in Debora's room for the last night. An opened bottle of Roederer Brut Premier champagne welcomed them when they entered her room. Akshay closely watched the minimalistic but elegant decorations. Beds were spread across the floor to occupy them; Saesha chose the cot, Abhinav sat on the bean bag, while Akshay occupied the bed, lying on the floor along with Debora.

"Cheers to Montreal". All of them raised a wine glass and kickstarted the party.

After a few minutes, people spoke about their memorable experiences in Montreal. Akshay was mindfully listening to every experience and wondered what he would narrate. It was Akshay's turn next.

"I can't pinpoint a single experience. All my Montreal experiences were remarkable. This is my first international experience, and I am glad it happened with you guys. Parties, nightlife, food exploration, dance workshops, the Toronto trip, and unexpected adventures all surprised me. I will miss each one of you. So stay in touch, and if you are coming to India, count on me"!

Akshay consumed another glass of wine and continued listening to others. Later, they played card and board games like Monopoly while sipping more drinks. While all this, Akshay reflected on his past Montreal days. All the moments he shared with Saesha were beautiful, the most colourful days of his life.

"When I return from Montreal, this happiness will translate to pain, which I must overcome as soon as possible". Akshay made up his mind to be more mindful of reality.

"Will you miss Abhinav"? Akshay asked Debora amidst this confusion. "I think, yes. But I don't think he will". She laughed.

"Why do you believe so"?

"Maybe I am more emotional among the two of us". She replied

Akshay remained silent for a while. Then, finally, Debora looked into his eyes and spoke.

"I think I know what you are thinking. You will miss Saesha".

Akshay: "Yes, I will".

Debora: "Will she miss you"?

Akshay: "Definitely".

"Saesha, will you miss Abhinav? Sorry, Akshay"? Debora shouted to the crowd.

"Yes, I will miss Akshay, I will miss Abhinav, I will miss Debora…. "The sloshed Saesha lying on the bed continued popping out names of the people in the room.

Debora laughed. "Why are you laughing"? Akshay asked her.

Debora: "She misses you generally and not specifically".

Akshay: "That's fine. Your question was whether she would miss me or not".

Debora: "Okay, now answer me. Are you in love with Saesha"?

Akshay: "No, I don't; I mean, I don't know…"

Akshay loves Sa… Debora shouted again. Akshay closed her mouth this time and requested, "Please shut your mouth".

CHAPTER TWELVE

LUCKY BREAK

A few hours later, Akshay bid goodbye to everyone. His airport cab was waiting at the parking lot. Saesha helped him carry the luggage to the spot, while others stayed back in Debora's room and continued playing the Monopoly game.

"Will you miss us"? He asked Saesha while walking to the parking spot.

"Indeed. We made our Montreal days special; thanks for always being there, Akshay! I wish you only good luck. I am not sure if you will be coming to Europe anytime soon. But I will make it a point to visit you in India". Saesha hugged Akshay and said, "I will miss you, my friend! Travel safe and stay in touch"!

"Sure, bye, stay in touch". Akshay entered the cab with mixed feelings and waved one final goodbye to her. Saesha waited at the parking slot until Akshay's cab left her eyesight. Post, he saw her running back to Debora's house party.

While traveling back, Akshay reminisced about his Montreal days for one last time and only felt gratitude. Two different continents and countries, poles apart social circles, dissimilar personalities, and contrasting outlooks towards life, there was absolutely nothing common between them. Yet, despite the differences, Saesha, an heir to billions, was a great companion to Akshay. Akshay felt as if he had woken up from a beautiful dream.

"Sir, all good"? The cab driver enquired.

Akshay noticed the driver. He wore a black woollen sweater, had a long beard, and a pleasant smile. The cab driver appeared to be someone from the Indian subcontinent.

"Yes.. yess". Akshay replied. "Or maybe… Actually No… but that's it about it", Akshay clarified himself.

"Are you from India"? Akshay asked, noticing his accent, skin tone, and dress code.

"Bengal", the driver replied.

"Kolkata"? Akshay wanted to confirm.

"No, Sir, I meant Bangladesh".

"Oh, Okay. Got it. My bad". Akshay learned that outside India, Bengal could stand for the land of Bangladesh or the formerly East Pakistan, which was partitioned into a separate country after the Independence of India from the British in 1947.

The driver smiled back at Akshay and continued his pleasant drive. The car had a unique fragrance similar to a traditional attar scent. How many years have you been in Canada? Akshay asked.

"It's been more than ten years now".

"Nice. What do you like the best about Canada"?

"Everything is good here, Sir". Akshay was surprised to hear such a complete answer.

"Don't you miss your home in Bangladesh"?

"Who doesn't miss their hometown, Sir"? The driver posed a question back at Akshay.

"Then why don't you go home"?

"It's not that easy, Sir"!

"Why not? Should I book a flight ticket for you to Bangladesh"?

The driver laughed at his innocence and replied. "Thanks for the ticket offer, Sir. But here, I have a respectful job and can feed my family give them good clothes, and education. Though I had to leave my hometown and be a refugee in this country, here I can live a life of dignity".

The serious tone of the conversations diluted the dopamine effect induced on his body by the farewell party; he turned half-sober. He also felt better that the shift of the conversations is keeping him better, though a snapshot of Saesha waving the final goodbye to him is popping up again and again at a regular frequency.

That image, that sight, that woman! OMG! Akshay screamed! The driver stopped the vehicle and saw a disturbed Akshay.

"You need some water to drink"? The driver asked.

"Haan, that would be helpful", Akshay replied.

The driver stopped the car, opened his trunk, and picked up two bottles of water bottles. He asked Akshay to drink enough water and wash his face so he could feel better for the rest of the journey to the Montreal airport.

"Your smile is beautiful, Sir. Retain that on your face always". The driver said. Akshay looked at the driver with a smile and hugged him tightly.

"Cool, I am good. Sorry to trouble you. Let's head to the airport before it gets late," Akshay apologised.

"Are you sure"?

"Yes, Pakka".

"Great"! the driver replied and started his car. The car drove silently before the conversations between both restarted.

Akshay: "Did you have a love marriage or an arranged marriage"?

Driver: "Arrange marriage, Sir".

Akshay: "Ohh, okay. And have you found love in your life"?

Driver: "Yes, Sir. I love my wife, and she loves me back".

Akshay: "That's great"!

Driver: "And now I have got a new person to love".

"Who is that"? Akshay was curious.

Driver: "My angel, my one-year-old daughter, Sir".

Akshay: "Ohh, yeah, gotcha! What's her name"?

"She is Emel, my adorable princess".

Akshay: "Nice name, rare too. You must be having a great family time".

Driver: "Yes, Sir. It's a Turkish name; she was born eight years after our marriage. So, we were looking for a rare name and finally found this".

Akshay smiled back at his happy life with a lot of content.

Driver: "Do you miss the girl who was waving her hand at you"?

Akshay: "Yes, very much. But how did you make out"?

Driver: "You were looking for her through the rear-view mirror till she disappeared".

Akshay: "Sir, you got the worth of my feelings in a minute, which she hasn't understood for the last sixty days".

Driver: "How do you know that she doesn't love you back"?

Akshay: "Because we discussed about it".

Driver: "Okay, at times, we men must push women".

Akshay: "I don't know, Sir, but I can tell she is not a regular girl who can be won through a normal push; she is one of a kind. She deserved to be desired and not conquered".

"Brother, you are in crazy love; I didn't mean to hurt your feelings".

Akshay didn't reply for a while.

"It is impossible to describe her; her face is sheer poetry, her smile is a haunting melody, her kindness is nothing like seen before.... yes, it is impossible to describe her". Akshay broke the silence in the car through his words. The driver realised that the teenager was madly in love with this girl and decided to be considerate of him and his emotions.

"What did she tell you when you left now"? the driver asked.

"Will stay in touch…".

"So, you can meet her back in India, right? What's the problem"?

"She doesn't stay in India, and her family runs a flower business in Florence, Italy. She is the only daughter of a multi-billionaire in Europe. I told her right, that she is a rare girl".

"Okay", the driver replied.

"Just let go of your wishes and accept the beautiful life that Allah has charted for you. Believe in him, and he will protect you. In your case, continue believing in your favourite god, like Ram or Krishna. Only good will happen to good people.

Never mind, we are reaching the airport in 5 minutes," The driver concluded his philosophical thought.

Upon hearing it, Akshay grabbed a Toblerone chocolate from his bag and passed it to the driver. "This is for your daughter. It is a small gift from my end. Please pass it on to Emel".

"Thanks, a lot, Sir. She loves chocolates".

"Ohh, that's nice to hear". Akshay was glad that Emel would love his Toblerone.

The driver gave his mobile phone to Akshay and told him it was Emel on his phone's wallpaper.

"She looks super cute. She sketches at this young age". Akshay was curious as the wallpaper image was that of Emel sketching on a white canvas.

"Yes, Sir, she is immensely talented. She has drawn hundreds of sketches so far. We wanted to collate all these paintings and sketches and conduct an exhibition in her name sometime. That's the biggest dream of mine and my wife". Driver said.

Oh no, she sounds like a prodigy. She deserves more than one chocolate.

Akshay searched his bag for something more she could pass onto Emel. He could only find a curated box of chocolates that Saesha had gifted him before leaving. He was double-minded about whether to pass it on to Emel, but that was the only gift he could gather from his bag. Without much thought, Akshay decided to share the chocolate box with Emel as he wished to delete all his memories of Saesha and move on with his new life back in India.

"That's so nice of you, Sir. I will talk about you to my wife and Emel, and they will be super happy".

Akshay smiled back. By then, they had reached the airport, and the driver stopped the car and assisted Akshay with his luggage from the trunk. He hugged the driver again and walked towards the airport entrance with his suitcases.

In a few seconds, Akshay turned back and asked the driver.

"What does the name Emel mean"?

The driver was in his seat with the reverse gear on. "Desire, Emel means desire in Arabic". He replied.

"This is my number. Text me what your daughter replies," Akshay replied with a blossomed face.

"Sure, Sir, but she is mute, she doesn't speak". The driver passed. He smiled and headed back in his car. Akshay stood in silence, passed a smile, and walked towards the board – "Welcome to the Montreal Airport".

* * *

Florence café. It was almost half past midnight. The café was still moderately crowded, and people enjoyed conversations through more food and more drinks. Life was seemingly happy everywhere, like Akshay's life. Akshay had finished narrating his story. There was an air of silence between them. He was waiting for Madhu to respond. But maybe his story demanded silence. Suddenly, Madhu broke the silence.

"What happened after Montreal"? Madhu also wanted to listen to the post-Montreal part. But Akshay remained silent. Madhu enquired again.

"Nothing, that was the end". Eventually, he replied.

"What do you mean by the end? When did you call her next after reaching India"? She was muddled on Akshay's reply.

"I have not spoken to her after Montreal", Akshay clarified.

Madhu: "What? Didn't you have her mobile number? How is that possible"?

Akshay: "Yes, I had. I tried to reach her on the phone many times after reaching India but failed every time. And she is not present on any social media platforms as she was before".

Madhu: "That's weird. There is something strange about everything you narrated".

Akshay didn't reply, but Madhu decided to help Akshay in all the best possible ways. Akshay had painted an ideal picture of a dream girl, and now, in Florence, Saesha's curious nature compelled her to investigate Akshay's past further.

"Akshay, we have more than a week left in this city. I will join you in the search, and we will find her. But what I am unsure of is why you want to meet her. She must have moved on! Sorry for being harsh, but that's what I can speculate from what I heard".

"Saesha was the most beautiful riddle I have encountered in life. She was an enigma; she came out of nowhere and dispersed into thin air, similar to the first moment I saw her during the street performance. The duration only got extended from a few seconds to over a month. And now, when I look back, those days in Montreal were the happiest days of my life. I initially thought it was a phase and I would overcome it. I waited days, months, and now years. Nothing changed; the Montreal memories are still afresh in my mind. I never thought those passing fancy Montreal days would excite me, go crazy, disturbed, and haunted simultaneously. And from what I have narrated, don't you think she is special enough to be searched for in this city"? Akshay articulated to his best. Having known Akshay, Madhu realised it would be hard for Akshay to push back from his thoughts and decisions.

"I know an Akshay who is boring as hell; otherwise, I would have fallen for you". Madhu tried to comfort Akshay through her sweet words, but he hardly responded.

"Okay, let's get back to the hunt. Where all have you searched so far"?

Akshay: "I tried contacting various flower business houses in Florence, but they hardly gave me any progressive leads".

Madhu: "What all information do you have about her"?

Akshay: "All I know is that she owns one of Europe's largest floral wholesaling businesses and is settled in Florence. With this information, I had multiple searches, but…"

Madhu: "Okay, now let me try from my end. I suspect it shouldn't be that difficult. In the worst case, I will try to seek help from our client. They should know the local influential business groups".

Akshay: "That was my last resort, too, but I hesitated to barge indirectly. If you can do it from your end, I would be highly thankful, Madhu".

Madhu: "Sure, why not? I should at least do that for you, man"!

Meanwhile, Akshay's phone rang, and he answered the call. "Hi, This is Akshay".

Akshay excused Madhu and left the table to attend the call. Madhu looked around the café; the loyal customers of the café were still enjoying their moments and every bit of life. They were living, not just existing. On this night, she could greatly appreciate Florence and this historic city's vibes to a greater extent. And in the same convoluted city, she is now supposed to search for another complex woman, Akshay's Florence girl.

"Saesha, age roughly 27/28, heir to one of Europe's largest floral business groups, settled in Florence".

"It shouldn't be difficult," She wondered. Meanwhile, after attending the call, Akshay returned to the table with thankful peace. "Who was on the call"? Akshay didn't reply to Madhu's question but wondered in silence. He was shaken, delighted, surprised, and contented. A myriad of emotions flew through his face.

"What happened? All good, Akshay"?

"Yeah. I just can't believe the call. Madhu. I will tell you something; I guess I finally got a lead in my search for Saesha," Akshay replied in full rejoice. "Really! What's the lead"? Madhu asked exhilaratingly. "It's unbelievable, to be bloody honest". Akshay took a long breath. "Tell me now"! Madhu was equally excited as Akshay.

"I am sorry, Madhu. I can't reveal it now". Akshay replied. "I am not leaving this place without you telling me who called you right now". She was crystal clear in her words.

"I will give you a clue. The Montreal story and the facts I knew have no connection with the lead, which means you can comfortably ignore everything I narrated. And that's the most surprising part for me"!

"How is that even a clue"? She actively protested. "Please wait a few more days; let me seek some clarity. And my heart says, if this leads me to Saesha, my story might have a happy ending". Madhu smiled in abundance at Akshay's reply.

CHAPTER THIRTEEN

A TALE OF TWO CITIES

Akshay didn't turn up in the office for the next two days. When enquired with the team, Madhu was informed that he had marked leaves. "Where did he go"? Madhu wondered.

Nobody within the team knew where Akshay had gone. Moreover, he didn't respond to Madhu's calls and text messages. Finally, on that day evening, she receives a call from Akshay.

Madhu: "Hey, Akshay, where were you? Why were you not answering the call"?

Akshay: "I am sorry, I got stuck".

Madhu: "Stucked up where? Did you meet Saesha"?

Akshay: "I will tell you everything in person. How about we catch up for dinner tonight"?

Madhu: "Yeah, sure. Text me the details; I will be there".

Florence, one of the world's best-preserved UNESCO cities, is famous for its traditional Tuscan cuisine. Some signature dishes include the Ribollita soup (a bread soup made with bread and vegetables) and bisteeca Fiorentina T-bone steak (an Italian steak made of veal or heifer). Apart from these traditional dishes, the street food culture has also picked up in the last few decades, leading to more dishes like lampredotto, an organic meat dish made from a cow abomasum's fourth and final stomach. This protein is slathered and sandwiched in a bread roll and sold through moving food trucks in the bustling squares of the city.

"Enoteca Pinchiori, 8:30 pm". Akshay texted Madhu the venue and time to Madhu.

Madhu was delayed by half an hour due to some pending work at the office, which she had informed Akshay about in advance. Once ready, she dressed in a velvet gown purchased in Florence, perfect for the dinner ahead. Arriving at Enoteca Pinchiori, one of the city's oldest and most renowned restaurants, Madhu spotted Akshay sitting at a table for three, accompanied by another person. Akshay caught her eye and waved her over, prompting Madhu to approach, curious about the identity of his companion.

As Madhu took her seat between Akshay and the mystery woman, she couldn't help but wonder about the significance of this unexpected guest in their evening plans. Madhu occupied the third seat between Akshay and the woman.

"Hey, Saesha, this is Madhu, my colleague and friend, and Madhu, this is Saesha, my friend". Akshay introduced both. "Hey, Madhu, nice to meet you"! Saesha looked young and vibrant and dressed in a simple white shirt and jeans. She resonated with the spirited vibes of a teenage girl that Akshay had narrated and the little mannerisms of a millionaire businesswoman. "Nice to meet you, Saesha. Akshay has spoken a lot about you", Madhu replied.

"Really? What all". Saesha was curious to know more. Madhu observed the beauty of her curiosity and replied. "He has told us that he has a special millionaire friend in Florence, which we hardly believed and mocked him regularly".

"That's one hundred percent true. Don't mock him anymore, please"! She patted Akshay's shoulders, observed his attire, and commented that his sense of dress had improved substantially. Akshay interfered between the conversations and enquired about their food preferences for the night. After finalising the order, Akshay and Madhu spoke about their Florence project to Saesha. At the same time, Saesha shared her amateur experiences of leading her family business forward and adapting to the changing times.

Conversations, food, drinks, and more conversations popped in. Madhu noticed Saesha to be special, as Akshay had narrated. An optimistic, intelligent, and enterprising young woman with an inherent strange charm.

A few minutes later, Saesha excused them for a while and left the table. An impatient Madhu wanted answers to many questions unravelling through her mind in the past forty-five minutes. "What is happening, Akshay? Is this why you waited so long to meet her"?

"I am sorry. I didn't get you", Akshay replied.

Madhu: "Why did you call me for the night? What's my role today"?

Akshay: "Nothing. I thought I would introduce you to Saesha".

Madhu: "That's it".

Akshay: "Yes, absolutely".

Madhu: "How did she react when you found her after years"?

Akshay: "She was delighted".

Madhu: "That's it. I need to hear the complete story".

Akshay: "Yeah, I will tell you after the dinner".

"Hey, I am sorry, guys, I caught up with something urgent and have to leave now. Busy days now, but I couldn't say no to him". Saesha returned, patted Akshay's hair, and asked, "Should I offer any lift to you folks"?

"No, we are good", Madhu replied.

"Are you sure, Akshay"? She looked at Akshay's straight face and cleared up.

"Yes, Saesha. I will call you. Take care," Akshay replied with a forced smile. Saesha smiled in return and walked out of the restaurant. Her driver was waiting outside; she entered the car and waved another goodbye to Akshay.

The restaurant housed only two more couples apart from Madhu and Akshay after Saesha left them. "Did you like this restaurant"? Akshay asked Madhu. "Yeah, it looks pretty different and traditional. Vintage types", Madhu replied.

Akshay: "I did not like the ambience much, and the food was also mediocre".

Madhu: "You chose the venue and menu".

Akshay: "I did choose the meal, but Saesha selected the venue".

Madhu: "Then you should have asked her before ordering the food".

Akshay: "Why are you trying to argue with me"?

Madhu: "I was stating facts, not arguing".

Akshay remained silent for a while. "What's your problem"? Madhu broke the silence on a softer tune.

Akshay: "I don't have any problem".

Madhu: "Okay, you don't have any problem. But tell me the complete story, right now".

Akshay: "Let's first leave this place. Our stay is within walkable distance from here; we can walk instead of booking a cab".

Madhu: "I am fine either way, provided you tell me what happened in the last two days".

Akshay: "Okay. Why are you so childish"?

Madhu: "I am not childish; you are".

Akshay: "Okay, no more arguments".

Akshay abandoned the leftover food and walked towards the exit door. Madhu followed him. The Florence roads unusually had fewer people and no street performances. Maybe the time has passed for one. Nevertheless, the silent city also had charm, elegant desirability, and attractiveness.

"Who called you that night"? Madhu was clear on the questions to be asked, but Akshay continued to be silent. "Okay, thanks for dinner; I am booking a cab and leaving now". Madhu attempted to leave while Akshay continued speaking, "The caller gave me Saesha's contact number, and I immediately rang her".

Madhu stopped, turned back, and replied, "Got her number so quickly? You searched for Saesha in every nook and corner of this city for over a month. And now, an angel gifts the number out of the blue".

"That's not very relevant", Akshay replied.

"Okay, continue, Sir"!

"Saesha was surprised to hear me on the other side. She was in Florence and wanted to meet me immediately. I also wished to meet her the same night, but she had put forward the plan before I proposed it. So, I was on cloud nine, and I couldn't believe that I was finally meeting her".

* * *

Saesha: "Akshay, how about we go for a night walk in Florence"?

Akshay: "You mean now"?

"Yes, reminiscing our Montreal nights". Saesha turned nostalgic.

Akshay's years of waiting finally concluded. After the Montreal nights, destiny has offered another opportunity for him to spend the nights with Saesha, and this time in the ethereal Florence. "So what all has changed from Montreal to Florence"? Akshay wondered.

Whatsoever, he expected to discover an energetic teenage form of himself, which had been dormant for a while in the coming nights. He had more than a month for self-discovery in Montreal, while his Florence days were counted as less than two weeks. Nonetheless, he decided to live and cherish every second of his Florence days.

CHAPTER FOURTEEN

ETHEREAL FLORENCE

"*Y*ou can spot me holding a yellow umbrella at Florence city centre Piazza Del Duomo".

Akshay's phone buzzed. Saesha texted this direction to Akshay for the meeting. Almost every European city had a city centre near the geographical centre and housed critical historic buildings. The city tours led by professional guides for the tourists mainly originated from these city centres.

This city centre is part of quarter one of Florence. This entire quarter premise is part of the UNESCO World Heritage Sites. Every year, this city attracts millions of visitors who take part in the splendour of the Duomo (The Florence Cathedral), browse the art at the Uffizi gallery, and walk the Ponte Vecchio. The Ponte Vecchio is a medieval stone-closed arch bridge built over the Arno River. It locates many shopping outlets like jewellers, art dealers, and souvenir sellers. The Piazza Del Duomo square, which Saesha texted, is the most visited area in Florence. It contains the Florence Cathedral and the Florence Baptistery, and many other important buildings surround it.

Akshay walked towards the square, which was a ten-minute walk. The roads were predominantly empty except for a few cafes and nightclubs, which were still operational. On his stroll, Akshay recalled the Montreal night adventures and the insane amount of fun they had.

Akshay was closer to the square, surrounded by historical and cultural heritage sites, which speak volumes about European medieval history. He could sense his heartbeat aloud. Yes, a white lady was holding a yellow umbrella at the corner. Akshay walked closer to her; a few seconds later, Saesha recognised Akshay. She hustled towards Akshay with a broad smile and embraced him. "What's up, young man"?

"I am only surprised"! Akshay replied.

"Me too; looks like a dream; it's been pretty long," Saesha agreed with Akshay.

"Yes, unbelievable, right"?

"Yeah. She gasped and continued, "How are you? What brings you to Florence"?

"I am good. The job keeps life busy. And my work brought me here. I have been on a consulting project for the last few months". Akshay replied. "That's amazing! You look pretty different and mature now," Saesha gestured to keep walking.

Akshay: "Really? It may be coming of age. But you look almost the same".

Saesha: "Haha, I am not sure if that was a compliment".

Akshay: "Yes, it was".

Saesha: "Thanks, Akshay! What do you want to do for the night? I am all yours".

Akshay: "Let's walk like this through the Florence streets".

Saesha: "Sure, I will show you the places around. We have about seven years of life to discuss".

"Yeah, seven years and nine months". Saesha was impressed by Akshay's accuracy.

Akshay: "So, what are you doing these days"?

Saesha: "I worked with the Red Cross for more than three years, and now, I could say I was on a break".

Akshay: "Who is running the family business then"?

Saesha: "Yeah, I also have that responsibility but have not fully delved into the business. The father is primary in charge".

Akshay: "Okay, and your mom"?

Saesha: "She is no more, Akshay".

Akshay: "Ohh, I am sorry; my heartfelt condolences".

Saesha: "It's been six months now. It was one of the difficult phases of my life, and it was challenging to bring the father to normalcy. He is doing much better now, and I am grateful for that".

Akshay: "That's good to know".

Akshay and Saesha continued walking through the streets, covering different historic buildings. First, Saesha explained the historical significance of the Florence Cathedral or the Duomo di Firenze (Italian). This gothic architecture cathedral was structurally completed in 1436 and had an elaborate ninetieth-century Gothic revival by Fabris, a famous Italian architect. The basilica's exterior is faced with marble panels in various shades of green and pink and is bordered by white. Next, they passed on other buildings like Giotto's Campanile, a fourteen-meter freestanding bell tower consisting of five stages in total, each adorned with intricate details and decorative elements that showcase the skill and artistry of its creators. Giotto's Campanile is a stunning example of Gothic architecture and a masterpiece of design and craftsmanship. The beauty of Giotto's Campanile lies in its elegant proportions and harmonious design. The tower's exterior is clad in white, green, and pink marble, creating a striking contrast against the blue sky. Elaborate sculptures and reliefs decorate the exterior, depicting scenes from the Bible and the lives of saints, adding depth and meaning to the tower's façade. At the top of Giotto's Campanile, visitors are treated to breathtaking views of Florence and the surrounding countryside. The beauty of the city's skyline, with its domes and bell towers, is a testament to Florence's rich history and cultural heritage, making Giotto's Campanile not just a bell tower but a symbol of the city itself. Saesha explained about the works of art and architecture embroidered on the tower.

"How do you know about the city in so much detail? I won't be able to explain any Indian city to you in this detail". Akshay was awestruck at the detailing of Saesha's explanation.

"Earlier, I used to work part-time as a city tour guide. The square where we met was the starting point of my city tours. It is bringing a lot of nostalgic memories to me". She lit a Nat Sherman charcoal filter cigarette with a gold filter tip and passed on one to Akshay.

"That's incredible. So, are you going on a night city tour with me"? Akshay tried to pull her leg after lighting his cigarette.

"Yeah, but you need not pay me; I am offering you a free one", Saesha smiled. "It is a fun job; you meet many new people, exchange ideas and perspectives, and learn and unlearn more about this beautiful city," She continued.

They walked further in silence before Akshay interrupted the calmness. "I tried contacting you many times after reaching India but failed every time".

"I know, right? I lost my phone at Montreal airport while traveling back to Brussels. And hence all the contacts. I always wondered if we would meet again in life". This clarification from Saesha was an excellent relief for Akshay.

Saesha: "How did you get my contact number now"?

Akshay: "That's an unbelievable story".

Saesha: "Tell me".

Akshay: "No way you hear it out of my mouth. You will get to discover it yourself soon".

Saesha: "Are you sure"?

Akshay: "Yes, I hope so".

Saesha: "Okay, I will keep waiting then".

"Do you remember how you loaded me with surprises in Montreal? It's my turn now in Florence". Saesha laughed at hearing Akshay's sweet way of revenge.

Saesha: "How long are you in Florence"?

Akshay: "Maybe a week more. I need to be back in Chennai for my cousin's wedding".

Saesha: "Will your work commitments be over by then"?

Akshay: "Yeah, it is completed now, it might have some ad-hoc work".

Saesha: "Okay. What plans are for next week"?

Akshay: "I haven't planned any. The past few years have made me a bit boring in life; after all, we are no longer the carefree college kids".

Saesha: "Yeah, true, those days were pretty simple. When in retrospect, those were the best days of my life".

"What else is happening in life"? Akshay was curious to know more about her.

"Extreme calmness, the one you have after a storm or a cyclone—moments of tranquillity. I have been undergoing many adventures in the last six years, but now I aim to take over the business from my aging father. He needs rest after mom's demise".

"Right, what do you mean by adventure"? Akshay wondered

"Love, marriage, and separation, the golden trinity". She took a pause and replied calmly.

"Why do you always surprise me with your life"? Akshay replied shockingly. Saesha laughed unexpectedly and continued, "Yeah, it was a challenging phase; I learned a lot! I am now ready to deal with life and its inherent challenges".

Akshay: "How did you meet"?

Saesha: "You want me to download the flashback"?

Akshay: "The night is young, and we have miles to go before we sleep".

"He was my colleague in the Red Cross, where I joined as a trainee after graduation. We were working out of the Genevan office. He was from Sevilla in Spain and of Moroccan descent. We worked on a few projects together, including one in Congo, Africa, where we got to know each other more. It was during the Congo days that he proposed".

"You are a pathetic storyteller. Do you remember how vividly I narrated mine in Montreal"? Akshay interrupted her narration. "Ha-ha, yeah. Let me improvise". She got excited and restarted the story.

"His name is Adam. He was two years older than me when I joined the Geneva office after my studies—a seemingly nice guy. There was a spark from the start. Our first interactions were part of the induction program. And the more we spoke, the more we realised how alike we were in our common interests. He was my go-to person in the office for all professional and personal assistance. Since I was new to the city, he helped me to familiarise myself with the super-expensive city of Geneva and its culture. And I hid from him the fact that I am rich. My inner voice just had a gut feeling".

"Interesting. I was waiting to hear that out". Saesha smiled at Akshay's reply. She paused. Akshay's eager eyes tempted her to go on.

Saesha: "A few months later, we were selected for an international child health assistance project in Congo as a part of a team of eight. It was a six-month schedule in Congo. Have you heard of Congo, Akshay"?

"Sorry, I know it is just another African country", Akshay replied, his hands taken from the jacket pockets.

Saesha: "Congo is in central Africa, one of the worst poverty-stricken African nations. It is extremely rich in natural resources but has been exploited poorly due to political instability, lack of basic infrastructure, and exuberant corruption by the colonisers and ruling governments for centuries. As a result, almost two million children starve every year, and the ongoing fighting has displaced more than four million people. The people's struggles and the country's atmosphere reminded me of the Sri Lankan civil war days my parents had narrated. However, the on-ground situation was more disturbing, which I can't describe through words".

Akshay: "Hmm, that's saddening".

"Every day, we gathered more courage to solve the people's problems and worked harder. One of the most meaningful six months I had spent, where I garnered maximum work satisfaction. We strategised various plans to effectively implement the aid received from five developed nations in tackling malnutrition in children". Saesha shared the photographs of her and Adam with the kids in Congo with Akshay.

"Adam and I were always together; we gradually realised that our relationship had discovered new definitions and meaning from being good friends and amazing colleagues. We didn't explicitly speak about it, but we knew it. Those were simpler, beautiful times, the moments of happiness". She stopped for a while, took a break for thirty seconds, and continued.

"After six months, we boarded the return flight from the Kinshasa airport in Congo to Geneva. Adam was sitting next to me. When the flight took off, Adam asked me, "Will you marry me"?

"I was surprised. I have never heard of any unusual proposal other than this in my life. The moments when I sensed butterflies in my stomach, I felt chosen in life and said an immediate yes. I was about to turn twenty-four in three months then. I wondered if that's too early to get married. But then, is there any right age to get married? After reaching Geneva, I was concerned about how I would pitch the idea of marriage to my parents".

Akshay: "What was your parents' response"?

Saesha: "Adam was a nice guy, and as expected, my parents didn't have any solid reasons to object to the marriage".

"Go ahead with your decision, my princess. We know you will only choose wisely because we trust you". My father whispered into my ears after introducing Adam at my home.

"I believe there were many similarities in our love stories. We discovered our love in similar socio-political environments in Congo and Sri Lanka. They eloped from Sri Lanka to Europe, while Adam proposed to me on the flight from Congo to Europe. Hence, I dreamt of marrying in the Florence Cathedral, where my parents wed decades back. Although, it was a simple and beautiful function attended by close relatives and friends. I felt like a queen that day; it was surreal!" Saesha shared her wedding photographs with Akshay from the phone.

"After our marriage, both of us continued to work with the Red Cross and was working out of the Geneva office for the next year. I wished to start a family and was excited to be a mother. In addition, the experiences of interacting with many kids in Africa and other places roused my curiosity about having a child. Finally, at age twenty-five, I became pregnant, and we were super excited about unleashing the next phase of our life. I moved to my parents' house in Florence while Adam stayed back in Geneva for work".

"Have you ever been pushed off a cliff to a sea, Akshay"?

"No. Never. Why do you ask that"?

"I have been. That was how I felt on that fateful day when my whole life took a U-turn. That morning, I sensed severe abdominal pain and was taken to the hospital by my mom and driver. I bled in the car. The most terrible pain of my life. Eventually, it resulted in a miscarriage at the hospital. I was two months then". She stopped for a while and continued.

"I felt I lost something vital from my body; I was diminished physically and mentally to a lesser entity. There was a great vacuum in my mind. You may call it anxiety, depression, post-traumatic disorder, etc. Whatsoever the name is, I wish none go through such a scenario in their lives".

Akshay was upset, disturbed, and horrified after hearing from Saesha. Of all the scenarios in which he would have expected to meet Saesha, Akshay wouldn't have even considered this.

"Where is Adam now"? Akshay asked.

"He is no more, Akshay. Two weeks later, Adam passed away in a road accident on the outskirts of Florence city". Saesha was in tears.

Akshay: "Oh my God! Saesha, I am sorry, I was not aware of any of these".

"Yes, Akshay. I am at mental peace now. The storm has passed on. At age five, God was extremely kind to me when my life took a turn for the best. Now, the same God is balancing out my blessings. That's how I took it to be. I realised it was not a logical statement, but it gave me hope to live with ambitions and desires". Saesha passed on a triumphant smile and replied.

Akshay: "Yeah, I understand. I never thought I would meet you like this in Florence".

"Why don't we stop and have some drink? I see a café opened there". She pointed towards a small café cum nightclub where they ordered a can of Hoegaarden beer each. The vintage melancholic city lights of Florence resonated with the yellow-coloured beer.

"That's how life is, Akshay. We don't have any control or idea of what life has stored for us in the future, making life exciting". She sipped more beer.

"After Adam's death, I quit my job at Red Cross. There was a greater void in life; the future was bleak. I wanted to stay away from Florence for a while, and one day, I took a backpack and left home with no plans. I travelled to the Scandinavian countries, camped there for weeks in a few wildlife sanctuaries, stayed closer to nature, and saw the Northern Lights. That trip continued to more countries, interacted with many people, picked up new hobbies like sketching, learned to play tunes on a Ukulele, and read indefinitely.

Initially, I saw no visible difference from these travels, but gradually things started falling into place. Finally, I could sense myself recovering and moving ahead in life. Happiness is a choice, and you have to opt for it, Akshay".

Akshay: "I am at a loss of words, Saesha. Before you narrated everything, you appeared the same Saesha I met in Montreal eight years back, and that's a brilliant sign. Hats off! I am glad that you could overcome those miserable days".

Saesha: "Thanks, Akshay. Now it's time for your turn. How were your past eight years"?

Akshay: "If your eight years were a TV series, mine would be just an episode".

Saesha: "In the sense"?

Akshay: "There was nothing eventful that happened in the last eight years".

Saesha responded with a disagreement.

"Nothing eventful happened; of course, I lived so many years. Once I was back in India from Montreal, my friends commented that I had changed for the better. I sensed much more confidence in experimenting with a lot of things. I became more participative in college extracurricular activities without any inhibitions. In short, I had a momentous two years of college life. After graduation, it was more or less a monotonous life; work, eat, sleep, and repeat, were absorbed into the vicious corporate cycle. Almost six years have passed since then, and now I am savouring beer with my old friend Saesha in this beautiful city. He tossed the beer up".

Saesha: "I am jealous of you, Akshay"!

Akshay: "Why? He was surprised".

Saesha: "How come you always tell me such beautiful life tales"?

Akshay: "The grass is always greener on the other side".

Saesha smiled.

Saesha: "But I expected another romantic anecdote, a better version than your teenage chronicle".

Akshay: "You still remember everything? Amazing memory you possess".

Saesha: "I know, right? But you didn't answer me".

Akshay: "No, I don't have any newer update".

Saesha: "Not even one".

Akshay: "No".

Saesha: "How is that even possible? That is not the Akshay I know of".

Akshay: "Legend says seven people in the world look alike. I tried searching for the rest of the six but in vain. Let's head back home".

Saesha: "Sure, I will call my driver; first, he will drop you and then I will return home".

Akshay: "Okay, Thanks".

The driver came in five minutes. Both entered the car. Akshay's stay was close by. It was a silent drive of about ten minutes, but the longest.

Saesha: "It was nice meeting you, Akshay. I felt relieved after talking to you. I wish you stayed here longer".

"Do you know what scares me the most? Am I destined to lose my near ones forever? Loneliness… Firstly, my parents, then the love of my life, and now we will also get separated in our lives soon. I wish I could grab all of you close to me till my death," She paused and continued.

Akshay: "I will meet you soon, Saesha. Let's plan something in the remaining days".

Akshay wanted to speak more, but he could not, so he reached his place of stay.

CHAPTER FIFTEEN

PLEASANT SURPRISE

"Did you meet Saesha after that"? Madhu asked eagerly, her curiosity piqued by Akshay's captivating narration of his recent night with Saesha.

"Not yet, but I plan to in the coming days", Akshay replied. Madhu was at a loss for Akshay's words.

Madhu: "She just looked cheerful and full of life. It's hard to believe what you told me about her".

Akshay: "Yeah, it was a bolt from the blue for me. It's hard to digest, and I feel relieved to have shared it with you. I am glad that you joined us for dinner".

Madhu: "Yeah, I understand, Akshay. Whatever, I think your riddle has been solved, and you can be in mental peace now".

Akshay: "Yes, meeting her in Florence has brought me some peace. But at the same time, I didn't expect to see her in this state here. To those who don't know her story, she seems fortunate, but if you delve deeper, you realize she has endured more than both of us combined. Life can be unfair, don't you think"?

Madhu: "Happiness is a choice; you must opt for it in life". I don't think you phrase it better than Saesha. She is a unique woman".

Madhu booked a cab to head back.

Madhu: "So, what's your plan now"?

Akshay: "I am working tomorrow. I plan to finish all my pending tasks and spend time with Saesha until I leave for India".

Madhu: "That's nice. Have you made any plans"?

Akshay: "Yeah. I want to spend time with her. I want to take her back to the Montreal days; I want her to smile, laugh, and cherish life".

Madhu: "I think she is already in a relaxed state".

Akshay: "Okay, but I guess I can be an excellent companion to cherish her happiness".

Madhu: "Yes, you can. So, when are you meeting her next"?

Akshay: "I think mostly the day after, for dinner. She has planned a surprise for me".

Madhu: "How can she be a box of surprises"?

Akshay laughed and replied. "I get you".

Madhu: "I hope this time it is a pleasant surprise".

Akshay: "Yes. She said she had planned a cute, little, and innocent surprise".

Madhu: "That again sounds interesting. What do you think the surprise would be"?

Akshay returned a winning smile in reply. He had two days and a night left to ponder the delightful surprise Saesha had in store for him in Florence.

CHAPTER SIXTEEN

THE ART AND THE ARTIST

Akshay spent the next day completing all his pending work and working ahead of his schedule. Saesha was also busy with some of her business meetings. She planned to meet Akshay the next afternoon in the Galleria dell Accademia in Firenze, which translates to the Academia Gallery of Florence. This museum is well known as the home of the celebrated artist Michelangelo's sculpture David. Created in 1504, David is a marble statue of the Biblical figure David and is considered a Renaissance masterpiece. The powerful warning eyes of David were fixated on Rome, the powerhouse centre. Apart from David, the museum houses many other sculptures and an extensive collection of paintings by the artists of the Florentine era.

Akshay located the museum and stood in the queue to collect entry tickets. He messaged Saesha to know if he should order tickets for her.

"I am inside; come nearby, David". She texted back.

Akshay: "Who is David"?

Saesha: "You will get to see him".

Akshay collected the entry ticket and hurried. Many wall paintings, sculptures, and statues of varying sizes were on both sides of the walkway from different periods. Each art form had a placard describing the artist, the history of the art, and its relevance. The crowd sauntered among these creative outputs with no hassle. Akshay's thoughts about David and Saesha were superseded once he entered the museum vanished. Instead, he was attracted by the marvellous beauty of a marble sculpture located meters ahead of him and walked straight in that direction. He thoughtfully scanned the seventeen-foot-tall statue before noticing "Michelangelo's David" written on a signboard adjacent to the statue.

"How is David"? Akshay heard Saesha's voice from his left.

Akshay: "Hey! Yeah, he is terrific, a fine piece of art".

Saesha: "He is the soul of Florence"!

Akshay: "Was this your surprise"?

"Yes". She agreed reluctantly.

Saesha: "Why? Aren't you excited"?

Akshay: "I am sorry, I had higher expectations. The sculpture is brilliant, but I could have easily googled to know about David and met him here in Florence. I was expecting something locally astounding".

Saesha: "Okay, maybe turn towards your right and look at that munchkin".

Akshay turned towards his left as instructed, "Emel darling, come", Saesha shrieked.

Akshay saw an eight-year-old little girl running towards Saesha. The cute little girl had a bag on her shoulders and smiled at Akshay. Akshay smiled back at her. "Akshay, here is my surprise. Meet Emel, my latest best friend in the town".

"Her name is Emel"? Akshay surprisingly asked.

Saesha: Yeah, what happened?

"Hi Emel, nice to meet you, young girl; I am Akshay" Akshay didn't respond to Saesha but introduced himself to the little girl. She smiled and gave a handshake in return. "She doesn't speak. She is mute, Akshay". Saesha warned him. "Ohh, I am really sorry". Akshay closely watched the little girl; she had a constant smile on her face.

Akshay: "Why is she carrying a bag"?

Saesha: "She is a fantastic artist; I would describe her as a prodigy. She carries her sketching book with her all the time in her bag".

Akshay: "Woah, that's amazing"!

The three moved around the museum, appreciating more artwork from the Renaissance period. Saesha posted the question, "Are you dating Madhu"?

"Madhu"? Akshay laughed. Emel also stared into Akshay's face from below. She was walking in the middle of both, with one handheld to each of them. "Yeah, she looks good, and I think you both would be a great pair," Saesha continued.

Akshay: "Really? She is already engaged, and her wedding is three months away".

Saesha: "Ahh, does that hurt you, Akshay"?

Akshay: "Why should it hurt me"?

Saesha: "Relax, I was trying to pull your leg like before".

Akshay smiled as a response to Saesha. He caressed Emel's hair, which she enjoyed while walking. Akshay and Saesha walked around the museum at the pace of the little girl. She stopped at pieces of art that she found enchanting and clicked their photographs using her mobile phone. "How did you meet Emel"? Akshay was curious.

Saesha: "That's a great story. As part of my business travel, I was in Paris a few weeks back and decided to visit the famous Louvre museum".

Akshay: "The iconic inverted pyramid museum mentioned in Dan Brown's work"?

"Yeah, the same. He alleges that the remains of Mary Magdalene are located under the inverted pyramid, which can be found in the Louvre's underground shopping centre. Apart from the mystery element, this museum is home to the celebrated painting Mona Lisa by Leonardo da Vinci, another masterpiece from the Renaissance period. I also discovered this angel on that visit to meet the beauty". She pointed towards the little girl who was busy capturing the Palestrina Pieta sculpture on her phone.

"She sat alone in a quiet corner of the Napoleon courtyard, a gentle smile lighting up her face as our eyes met. Intrigued by her presence, I approached and inquired about her guardian, but she signalled that she was alone. As I asked more questions, I realized she was mute, lost in the bustling crowd of the Louvre. I was worried and decided to find her parents with the help of the museum security team. I waited long without any progress as I couldn't leave her alone.

While we waited, she took out a painting book and quickly sketched a chapel, indicating it was her home. With the assistance of a security officer, we identified the chapel as the American Church in Paris, near the Eiffel Tower. Providing my details to the security team, I requested permission to take her to the Church. I carried this munchkin into my arms and drove towards the Church, where she recognized it as her home and led me to the reception. The reception team warmly welcomed her as Emel, one of the few children growing up in the children's assistance home attached to the Church".

"She is an orphan"? Akshay asked.

"Yeah, it took me two decades back; I saw a five-year-old myself in her. I looked into her glowing eyes with mixed emotions; she didn't stop smiling". Saesha kissed the forehead of the adorable tiny girl deeply.

"I requested the Mother of the Church to grant permission to take her out for the next few days. We roamed around the city of Paris, where I took her to the Eiffel Tower and the Notre Dame Cathedral, cruised through the Seine River, and attended the musical concerts at the Saint Chapelle Church. I hope she had lots of fun". Emel nodded her head in agreement.

Saesha: "She is a gem, one of a kind".

"Like you, I mean by name". Akshay passed on a playful smile.

Saesha: "Don't be short of words, Akshay. I am flattered".

Akshay: "How did you bring her to Florence from Paris"?

Saesha: "Her school is closed for a week due to an ongoing renovation activity. Hence, I fought for permission from the Church to bring her to Florence. She is visiting Florence for the first time now".

Akshay: "Nice. How many more days will she be here in Florence"?

Saesha: "She has to leave by tomorrow".

By then, they had completed the museum visit and reached back to the beginning, near the David statue. Emel grabbed Akshay's hands and ran towards David. She wanted a photograph of her with David in the background and requested Akshay to capture one on her phone. Saesha was overseeing the moments from behind. "You became friends already"? She wondered.

Akshay: "Yes, I think. She is very friendly".

Saesha agreed with Akshay. They exited the museum and walked through the streets of Florence. Saesha's driver was nearby.

Saesha: "I will be out of town for two days, Akshay".

Akshay: "Are you heading to Paris to drop Emel"?

Saesha: "No, I will travel to Frankfurt to drop her off. The Mother from the American Church in Paris is in Frankfurt now for a religious convention. So I will drop her off in Frankfurt and travel to Aalsmeer".

Akshay: "Is that the flower marketplace that you mentioned"?

Saesha: "Yeah, the same; it seems you also have a remarkable memory. The peak spring season has begun and is a prime business period for us; remember, it is the largest flower auction in Europe"!

Akshay: "Yeah, I remember. When are you traveling tomorrow"?

Saesha: "Are you planning to surprise again by tagging along with me, like Toronto"?

Akshay, delighted like an energetic pup, replied, "Now since you know of my plan, it is no longer a surprise".

CHAPTER SEVENTEEN

RED ROSE GARDENS

*A*alsmeer is a town located 28 km southwest of the capital city of Amsterdam in the Netherlands. Situated in the North Holland province, it is referred to as the flower capital of the world and houses numerous nurseries and an experimental station for floriculture. Nestled amidst lush greenery and picturesque waterways, Aalsmeer exudes a tranquil charm that captivates the heart. The town's quaint streets are lined with traditional Dutch houses, their facades adorned with colourful flowers and creeping vines, creating a scene straight out of a fairytale. At the heart of Aalsmeer lies the stunning Aalsmeer Flower Auction, the largest flower auction in the world. Here, a sea of vibrant blooms creates a kaleidoscope of colours and scents, providing a mesmerising backdrop for lovers to wander hand in hand, lost in the beauty of their surroundings. In Aalsmeer, romance blooms like the flowers that adorn its streets, creating a magical and unforgettable experience for lovers seeking a romantic escape.

The itinerary for the next day was to fly from Florence to Frankfurt, drop Saesha at the Church, and then travel to Aalsmeer. That night, after reaching home, Akshay rang Saesha. He and his team members always planned for a road trip to Europe, which never materialised. So he planned to check the feasibility of converting the Frankfurt to Aalsmeer flight journey to a much-awaited five-hour road trip. Saesha was not very sure of the timelines, and she wanted some time to confirm. Akshay had fingers crossed for her decision. They flew from Florence to Frankfurt the following day and dropped Saesha at the religious convention centre.

"What's the plan that you have charted out, Saesha"?

"I checked for the feasibility of a road trip; it seems difficult", Saesha replied.

"Okay", Akshay replied in disappointment. "Let's head out for lunch and then travel on an afternoon flight to Amsterdam"? She attempted to cheer up Akshay.

Akshay: "Okay, but how do we travel from Amsterdam to Aalsmeer then"?

Saesha: "It is just half an hour away. We can travel on a train or book a cab from Amsterdam airport".

Akshay: "Sure, it makes sense".

They had their lunch at a casual restaurant named Ebbelwoi Unser, where they ordered a plate of the traditional dish, schnitzel (a thin slice of meat fried in fat), each along with a few drinks. After lunch, Saesha booked a cab to travel back to the airport. They waited patiently for its arrival. A 1965 model Rolls Royce convertible vintage green car stopped beside them in five minutes. The driver came out and passed on the keys to Saesha. "Here is the key, Madam".

Saesha thanked him, moved to the driver's seat, and asked Akshay, "Come in my friend; our cab has arrived".

"This has been the best surprise so far", Akshay exclaimed, marvelling at the Rolls Royce's green beauty. "Thanks, buddy! And now you need not leave Europe without being on a road trip", Saesha replied, moving towards the driver's seat and instructing Akshay to use Google Maps for directions. "Frankfurt-Bonn-Cologne-Essen-Arnhem-Aalsmeer. That's roughly what the route looks like", Akshay replied after setting up directions for the journey. "We're not taking that route, Akshay. There's a route via Hanau-Dortmund, part of the German Fairy Tale Route", Saesha corrected him as she changed gears.

"What's the German Fairy Tale route"?

"It is a 600 km route from Hanau in central Germany to Bremen in the north. It consists of many beautiful tourist attractions from the Grimm collection of fairytales compiled by the Grimm brothers in the nineteenth century. As a dedication to them, the German fairy tale society established this route in 1975 to identify the essential houses, buildings, and areas mentioned in the fairytales through road signs depicting the heart-shaped body and head of a pretty, princess-like creature".

"Okay. Are you aware of these fairy tales? I don't think I have read any", Akshay feared if he would be left out of the background info.

Saesha: "Me neither. But it doesn't matter; trust me, we will drive through a magical road".

Saesha's suggestion proved brilliant; Akshay was captivated by the breathtaking scenery along the historic road. Triangular-shaped houses adorned with a magical array of colours, majestic vintage castles, the Pied Piper Foundation honouring the legend of the Pied Piper, and street performances featuring characters from various tales all contributed to the enchanting atmosphere. Driving through this picturesque landscape on well-designed and constructed roads was a unique experience that Akshay wouldn't trade for anything.

Akshay: "I never thought such places existed in real. For me, it was in books or film production studios where they carved such locations to shoot the scenes. I wish I could read the German fairytales once and drive in this route again, wherein we could appreciate the beauty and the detailing to the fullest".

"I agree. Let's add to the bucket list"? She passed on a sly smile.

Akshay: "Are we still keeping a bucket list"?

Saesha: "No harm in having one, right"?

Akshay agreed with her optimism in life. After driving for two hours, they interchanged the responsibilities: Akshay as the driver and Saesha as the responsible shotgun. She followed the directions on Google Maps religiously and had a much better appetite for music that would suit a European road trip. So, the hours of happiness continued before they reached the Aalsmeer town by night around 8:30 pm.

The following day, Saesha took Akshay to the flower auction building of FloraHolland, the largest auction company in the world. The 10Mn sq. ft auction building is one of the largest commercial buildings in the world. The warehouse of the buildings constituted flowers of the likes of roses, lilacs, cyclamens, begonias, and freesias in large quantities. Saesha had a few meetings in the first half while she had arranged for Akshay to visit the warehouses and occupy himself in the first half of the building. After lunch, Saesha was free closer to evening, and they advanced to see the floral farms on millions of hectares.

"What a great business to operate! You are selling happiness to others; what else can make someone happy more than these bright red roses"?

"Yeah". Akshay noticed that the otherwise high-spirited Saesha was missing in her reply.

Akshay: "What happened? The morning meetings didn't go well".

Saesha: "I am good; the morning meetings went well".

Akshay: "Look at me. I can sense something is wrong with you"!

Saesha: "How can you be so sure"?

Akshay: "I think I know you pretty well. I can understand your emotions".

Saesha: That's a compelling statement with an overload of confidence".

Akshay: "Maybe, but I genuinely meant it".

Saesha: "Okay, then explain my current emotion".

Akshay: "You look a bit lost, more disappointment".

Saesha didn't reply but stared at Akshay with total contempt.

Akshay: "Okay, then please explain yourself".

It was another sunset in Aalsmeer, where the hues of the dusk were more oriented towards the red colour before heading to darkness, followed by more darkness. This reddish sunset resonated well with the red rose farms. As the sun sets over the tranquil waters of the Westeinderplassen, couples could enjoy a romantic boat ride, the gentle lapping of the water and the distant chirping of birds creating a serene and intimate atmosphere. But Saesha had a different perspective.

"What does this red colour remind you, Akshay"? Saesha posted back a question in reply.

"A rose farm, a beautiful sunset, a gorgeous woman beside me, this red only reminds me of love". Saesha laughed at Akshay's reply, but not the way Akshay had seen before. "Red, the colour of blood, stands for revolution". Akshay was perplexed at what Saesha was speaking about and where she was heading towards

"Here is the colour of the blood still; here is the smell of the blood still. All the perfumes of Arabia will not sweeten this little hand". Saesha replied calmly, without any melodrama.

Akshay: "What does that mean"?

Saesha: "That's a quote from the Shakespearean play, Macbeth, spoken by Lady Macbeth when she was overwhelmed by a fearful sense of guilt of the heinous crimes that she had encouraged Macbeth to commit, starting with the killing of King Duncan, the killing of Banquo and the murder of the Lady Macduff and her family".

"So"? Akshay was still baffled.

"Adam's death was not an accident. It was a planned murder, designed by me". Saesha replied.

Akshay: "What? Come again".

Saesha: "Yeah, what you heard is right".

Akshay: "All that you told was a lie"?

Saesha: "I just didn't lie to you, Akshay. I lied to the entire world".

Akshay: "Then, what's the truth"?

Saesha: "He was a bastard. Everything I narrated was true except for his death". Saesha broke off.

It was almost a month before my hospitalisation; Adam told me he was working with the Geneva office then. I trusted him. A few days later, I ran across him in a supermarket in Florence. I was all surprised. He explained he was replaced at the last moment in that project and thought he would spark a surprise visit to me later.

Saesha: "I sensed something wrong in his explanation. When I checked with the Geneva office, he was not part of any project late. I retrospected many similar incidents in the past where I doubted if I was made to believe a blatant lie. Day by day, my doubts about him inflated. I became restless. Adam was a divine messenger of hope for someone who had lost dear and near ones since her childhood. However, being carried, I had limitations, and I was not confident discussing my doubts with anyone, even my parents. With no other choice, I hired a private investigation agency to seek answers to my questions.

"Why did he lie to me? Where was he? What was he doing"?

"The professional agency submitted a detailed report with validated proofs within a week, and what I got to know was shocking; I was one of his choices. He was a womaniser who had relationships with multiple women".

"I seriously invested in our love, relationship, and our future baby with trust. What did I get in return? I was taken for granted. The agency report detailed a few cases of women trapped by him, and some were horrifying. The escalated mental tension became challenging to handle, and on that ruined day, my blood pressure shot up. I was rushed to the hospital but in vain.

It was days of silence from then for the next few days. I had no solid answers to my parents' continual question, "Where is Adam"?. Adam became aware of the agency I hired and stopped responding to my calls. I neither had replies to my parents nor the courage to inform my parents of the truth. That was the peak as well as the trigger point. I decided to put an end to everything! I rang up the agency and enquired about their comprehensive services. They redirected me to a contract assassin team, who executed the well-planned murder of Adam through a carefully designed unfortunate accident".

Akshay stood in shock!

Saesha: "That was a relief, moreover, an end to everything. I need not answer anyone's query, "Where is Adam"?

Akshay: "That sounds cruel".

Saesha appeared to be in disagreement with Akshay and turned against him.

Akshay: "I am sorry. I understand your hardships and sense of being cheated. Even then…"

"I don't know if what I had done is right or wrong; at times, the act haunts me, sometimes keeps me proud, while disturbs most of the times," Saesha interrupted.

Akshay didn't reply any. The atmosphere was no longer reddish and had proceeded to darkness on that new moon night. "If you were in my place, what would you have done, Akshay"? Saesha was curious.

Akshay was again silent for a while. Saesha trusted Akshay to share her biggest secret, but his minutes of silence troubled her and repented her action.

"Let's head back"? Saesha spoke and started making her way back from the farm. Akshay held onto her hand from behind. Saesha turned, and he replied.

"If I were as privileged as you, able to afford to hire someone to remove someone who hurt me from this world without facing the consequences, maybe then I would consider it".

Her smile was a work of art, her composure a melodious tune, and her defiance akin to a rebellious poet's. Akshay couldn't help but notice that the most captivating aspect of Saesha, which had intrigued and unsettled him for years, still remained: her sheer unpredictability!

As they walked away from the dimly lit red rose farm towards the parked car's headlights, Saesha smiled at Akshay, her hand still clasped in his.

CHAPTER EIGHTEEN

A BEACON OF LIGHT

The next morning, they dropped the car at Aalsmeer and onboarded a train to Amsterdam airport to fly back to Florence. "Who will take the car back to Frankfurt"? Akshay wondered.

"One of my staff will be traveling to Frankfurt next week from Aalsmeer. He will take it back then". She replied. "Okay. You seem to have a lot of connections in Europe", Akshay praised Saesha proudly. "I am building relationships now. It is imperative to run businesses across the continent".

"This is more grandeur than the most luxurious train I can afford in India". Akshay was in awe of the fast-paced, well-spaced, clean train with a decent WI-FI connection.

Saesha: "Have you travelled on a luxurious train in India"?

Akshay: "No".

Saesha: "Then, how can you compare"?

"Okay, that was supposed to be an exaggerated compliment to the well-built European railway network". Saesha smiled at Akshay and looked out through the window.

"Do you think I am a criminal"? She turned towards Akshay and asked all of a sudden. "Yes, you are; you committed a crime". Akshay replied with no second thoughts.

"Does that mean the law should punish me"? She appreciated Akshay's honesty and wanted to extend the conversation. "That's a tricky question. Justice and law may not always go hand in hand". His reply put Saesha into deep thought for a while, and she continued, "Are you now scared of me, Akshay"?

Akshay: "Hmm, the way you asked me makes me a bit uncomfortable".

"At times, I am traumatised by my actions and struggle to find peace in life. I was doubtful if I should share this with anyone. I felt comfortable talking to you and shared a heavy burden disturbing me". Saesha hugged Akshay on the train.

Akshay: "Am I the only person who knows about it"?

"Yes. Will you share it with anyone"? Saesha thought for a while and asked.

"I don't think so; I don't want to die in another car accident". Saesha stared into Akshay's eyes, and then both cracked into laughs. Akshay felt valued knowing one of her important secrets in life, though he didn't bother to explore its implications.

"Akshay, I need one more help from you. I am planning to adopt Emel into my life and my world. I love her so much, and I hope she loves me back. What do you think of it"?

"That's happily surprising. I mean, it is a bold move, and it has to be a thoughtful call. I hope you would have put enough brains into it before deciding".

Saesha: "Yeah, indeed. I introduced her to my Father and spoke with him about the same. He rested the final call to me. I also conducted an initial round of discussion with the American Church in Paris, and they considerably appreciated the decision with a clause. Emel's education is currently sponsored and will need their consent for the adoption. From my preliminary discussions with the Church, they suggested speaking directly with the sponsor and seeking clarification. Can you come with me to Paris for the meeting"?

Saesha ended with a request. She desperately wished Akshay would join her on the Paris trip but expressed only half her emotion.

"When is the meeting? I will have to leave Europe in the next few days".

"Ohh, I am sorry. I forgot about your cousin's wedding".

"Let's do this; I will reschedule my flight booked for next Saturday to Monday if we can visit Paris this weekend and schedule a meeting with the sponsor". Akshay devised a plan on the spot, and Saesha was impressed.

"Let me speak with the Church to mediate with the sponsor. Also, let's spend the weekend with Emel during the visit. She loves us. I was surprised that you befriended her quickly. In general, she is smart and intelligent but a shy girl," Saesha replied.

"Thanks to my experiences with my nephews and nieces at home, I have my ways to deal with kids," Akshay sounded confident.

"Nice. How many of them"? Saesha was curious to know more about his family.

"I have six nephews and nieces in total, and I try to send some gifts to all of them every year on important festival days. Very rarely do I get time to spend with them. So, I want them to remember me through my gifts". Akshay shared the photographs of his family with Saesha. She loved the gang of innocent kids. "That's lovely and shrewd at the same time", She remarked.

"Typical me".

"I knew you as a naïve person in Montreal but unsure of the tricky mindset". Akshay laughed at her compliment.

Akshay: "Maybe you will get to know me soon. Moreover, all of us have changed over time. By the way, are you sure the sponsor would agree to your decision? What if he disagrees"?

Saesha: "Why do you think he will disagree"?

Akshay: "I was only suggesting an option".

Saesha: "From what I gathered from the Church, the sponsor has no authority over the kid, so I think it should be possible to convince him. He can sponsor any other child instead of our Emel".

"Our Emel", You already seem to own her". Akshay passed on a light comment.

"Yeah, you are right. Hence, I don't even prefer to consider the scenario that you mentioned. It bothers me, worries me, and scares me"!

CHAPTER NINETEEN

LAST PAINTING

One of the most diverse and sophisticated cities globally, Paris is home to The Eiffel Tower, gorgeous landmarks, monuments, spacious boulevards, world-class shopping experiences, museums, art galleries, and charming cafes. With one of the most robust café cultures in the world, there is nothing more gratifying than sitting on a recliner chair at an outdoor café in Paris, sipping a coffee and eating a croissant while watching the famous sights that are constantly shown in travel magazines, movies and almost all pieces of art.

The meeting with the sponsor was fixed for Saturday in the American Church in Paris' office. Akshay and Saesha booked a morning flight from Florence to Paris and reached the Church around 2 pm. They decided to visit Emel before the meeting with the sponsor. Emel was well dressed in a bright red dress, and she rushed towards them from her room with her painting book. Saesha bent on her knees, welcomed her into her forearms, and hugged her tightly. How are you, sweetheart? Emel expressed her happiness with a wide nod. "Have you told her"? Akshay asked Saesha. She replied No.

"Why? I think you should have told her first". Akshay questioned her decision.

"I am afraid to give her false hopes and can't afford to see her tears. Years back, I have been there and can understand the delight of having someone care for you. It's a strong belief that will give you the confidence to gain heights in life. First, let's clear the official formalities and then break the news to her".

"Fair enough", Saesha's argument appeared reasonable to him. Akshay waved hands to Emel, and she happily extended a shaking hand. Then, the church office directed them to a meeting hall on the fourth floor. Emel also accompanied them. They exited the lift and walked through a narrow passage to enter a circular meeting hall.

"I will be back in a while" before heading to the passage, Akshay spoke.

Saesha passed a gesture asking, "Where"? and he pointed towards the washroom. Saesha and Emel continued walking through the passage to the hall, which contained transparent glass windows that offered a great view of the city of Paris and the lofty Eiffel Tower. Emel was attracted by sight and rushed towards the window after dropping her painting book on the circular meeting table. Saesha occupied one of the seats, opened the painting book, and glanced through her paintings from the beginning. Saesha had painted all the pages of the book except the last. So Saesha went through them one by one till the end with paramount inquisitiveness.

Meanwhile, Akshay walked into the hall from behind through the passage. Saesha listened to his footsteps and turned behind.

Akshay smiled at her. She stood from the chair, folded her arms, and glared at Akshay confidently. "What happened, Saesha"? Akshay asked her.

"This was your climax surprise"? She replied.

"Ahh, yes. I wanted to surprise you for one last time before leaving for India". She continued her glare at Akshay's reply.

"But how did you come to know about it"? Akshay was still unclear on what happened. Saesha didn't reply but passed on Emel's painting book to Akshay. Akshay went through the paintings.

"I can't believe that she did all this". Akshay stood in astonishment for a while before Saesha raised her query. "When did you meet Emel first"?

"After reaching Florence, I tried searching for you with all possible information available. I tried contacting various flower retailers and business groups, but no trace was available. During those down-on-luck days, I attended a weekend painting exhibition in Florence. I never thought that decision would have an impactful change in my life. While scanning through the artworks, I saw a painting that reminded me of the "Weeping Woman" by Pablo Picasso. A detailed abstract oil on canvas painting that explored numerous emotions. Out of eagerness, I scanned through the painting and saw a signature "Emel" written in the bottom right corner. I was wonderstruck. The last time I heard this name was when I unboarded my taxi to the Montreal airport at the end of the semester exchange. I had a long conversation with the taxi driver back then, where he spoke volumes about his family and his one-year-old daughter Emel, a great artist and mute. When I saw the name Emel, all those memories evoked me.

Curious to know the creator, I inquired with the exhibition staff beside me. He pointed his finger towards a happy little kid, who stood on my right next to the painting. She was happily looking at me, enjoying her creation. I bent down and asked her name, but she continued smiling.

The exhibition staff informed me that she is mute. I was dispirited for a while, but her perennial smile energised me. I wanted to meet her parents; the staff notified me that her guardian was standing next to the corner ahead. I walked towards the corner and saw the Mother from the Church interacting with people. After listening to her, I genuinely wanted to do something for her and expressed the same to the Mother. Since Emel was not a normal kid, they incurred a significant expenditure to fund her interests and take her to art exhibitions across places. So, the Mother was looking for sponsorship for her education and the growth of her talent".

Saesha looked towards Emel, who appreciated the city's beauty through the glass windows.

"Are you saying it's the same kid of the driver you met in Montreal"? Saesha was surprised.

"I don't know. I really wished that was not the case, as I couldn't imagine that beautiful human being living away from his daughter for any reason. That thought destroyed me. I decided if it was the same Emel, I really wanted to do something more for her apart from gifting her Toblerones. But there was no way to verify it.

Nevertheless, I decided to help her in any little possible way I could," Akshay replied.

"In your expedition to meet the enigmatic beauty Mona Lisa in Louvre, you met this darling, similarly; in my journey to discover my beloved angel, I stumbled upon her. Nothing but destiny, what time has carefully preserved over the years". Saesha listened to Akshay's narration patiently, and he noticed her turning emotional.

"Did you get my contact number from the Paris Church"? She questioned in a poignantly cracked voice.

"Yes, you are right. After you expressed interest in adopting Emel with the Church, the Mother immediately called me. Then, I was on a dinner with Madhu in Florence, narrating our Montreal days to her. The Mother texted me the details upon asking more about you.

Saesha Jayawardene, C/O of Venus Floral Enterprises, Florence,

Ph:055 306232

I became ecstatic. I never wondered if this cute little angel would be pivotal in my strenuous search for you. Moreover, she is a fantastic actor; she never gave you any hints. She played her role smartly, like a true artist".

Emel, who had appreciated the city's beauty through the windows till then, turned towards Akshay and Saesha, formed a heart symbol with her tiny hands, and smiled. Then, Saesha, in delightful tears, embraced Akshay and spoke.

"Akshay, I want you to be there with me for the rest of my life". Akshay pushed her front to his sight and surprisingly asked, "You mean you want to chant prayers with me".

"Yes". She replied, looking into his eyes. Akshay nodded a yes with an overload of happiness.

Saesha: "Promise me this is forever".

Akshay: "Yes, again, I don't want to meet death in a car accident".

Observing Akshay and Saesha share a kiss, Emel hurried to her chair and opened her painting book. Each page was a vivid depiction of Akshay's journey, from his flight from Chennai to Montreal to his first meeting with Saesha during a university street play, their shared moments cooking pasta in the kitchen, late-night walks in Montreal, visits to pubs and restaurants, and a poignant scene of Saesha on a roadside bench beside Akshay. The paintings captured the beauty of a Mont-Royal sunrise, lively Toronto nights, and their intimate tango dance.

The final pages depicted Akshay bidding farewell to Saesha from a moving car near the parking lot, their nights in Florence illuminated by city lights, the road trip from Frankfurt to Aalsmeer culminating in a vibrant sunset, and a touching scene of Saesha, Akshay, and the little girl in front of the American Church in Paris. Each frame was a masterpiece, showcasing Emel's talent and capturing the essence of their journey together. The last page remained blank, a symbol of the endless possibilities that lay ahead.

She rushed to the final page of her painting book, eager to capture the moment of Akshay and Saesha sharing their affection against the backdrop of the Eiffel Tower in Paris, the city of love. However, the innocent girl was unaware that destiny had planned an alternate ending.

CHAPTER TWENTY

THE GREATEST PRAYER

*T*he Piazzale Michelangelo sunset is the most enchanting view of the sunset in Florence or maybe in the world. It offers one of the city's most breathtaking views, especially during sunset. As the sun begins to dip below the horizon, casting a warm golden glow over the cityscape, the skyline of Florence transforms into a magical panorama.

From this vantage point, iconic landmarks such as the Duomo, Palazzo Vecchio, and Ponte Vecchio are illuminated by the soft evening light. The Arno River meanders through the city, reflecting the colours of the sky, creating a scene straight out of a painting.

As the sky changes hues from vibrant oranges and pinks to deep purples and blues, the city below comes alive with twinkling lights. The serene and peaceful atmosphere makes it a perfect spot for reflection and contemplation. Witnessing a sunset from Piazzale Michelangelo is not just a visual experience but a spiritual one, leaving you in awe of the beauty and grandeur of Florence.

A pleasant walk up the hill for ten minutes will lead you to this incredible location from the Florence city centre. Akshay and Saesha climbed up the hill by sipping a gelato each. Gelato is a frozen dessert of Italian origin made with a base of butterfat, whole milk, and sugar. It is denser and more prosperous, distinguishing it from other ice creams. Many outlets selling homemade gelato and other desserts are spotted while climbing the steps towards the sunset point.

After finishing the gelato, they found a place among the crowd to witness the sunset. People of all ages and cultures filled the sunset point and listened to the Italian street artists and musicians. Apart from the musical performances, many artists drew caricatures and paintings and narrated stories to kids.

"I miss Emel here. She would have loved this environment," Akshay remarked.

"Yeah, this place is very artistic. Next time, maybe", Saesha replied and moved a step closer to Akshay with a pleasant smile.

As the sun was setting, the crowd moved closer to capture the different hues of nature in its raw and purest form, but Akshay and Saesha preferred to be relaxed. They wanted to cherish the moment and stay back. Akshay recollected his fairy tale for a moment,

It all started with the Mont-Royal sunrise in Montreal and now ends with the Piazzale Michelangelo sunset in Florence. In this period of seven years, ten months, and twenty-five days, there were sunrises and sunsets every day, but I was never a part of it.

From this moment onwards, I will be an integral part of all the sunrises and sunsets.

Because I perceive these sun rays to be her magical touch.

Akshay looked into Saesha's eyes and chanted the world's most beautiful and greatest prayer.

Ti Amo *(Italian)*

Je Vous Aime *(French)*

Ik Houd Van Jou *(Dutch)*

Lch Liebe Dich *(German)*

Mama Oyata Adarei *(Sinhalese)*

Main Tumse Pyar Kartha Hoon *(Hindi)*

Naan Unnai Kadhalikiren *(Tamil)*

Jnan Ninne Snehikunnu *(Malayalam)*

I Love You

Piazzale Michelangelo shot on October 16th, 2019

The End

www.ingramcontent.com/pod-product-compliance
Lightning Source LLC
LaVergne TN
LVHW041605070526
838199LV00052B/2991